CROSSED IDENTITY

BY

GEOFFREY ODDS

Published By Geoffrey Odds
Cover Design: Tim Dorsett
ISBN: 978-0-9930769-1-6

CHAPTER 1

As the Boeing 737 turned into its final approach to Rhodes airport it glinted as the rising morning sun reflected from the polished metal of its wings and fuselage. John Hunter looked out onto the glimmering blue Aegean Sea and caught his first glimpse of the island. He needed a vacation and was looking forward to a full week's relaxation away from the pressures of business. This would be his first time vacationing in Europe; normally his vacations involved travelling back to Montana to see his parents for Thanksgiving and Christmas or maybe a long weekend skiing in Vermont. His work took him all over the world but gave him little time to see the places he visited. He was determined to make the most of this vacation, really relax and recharge his batteries, eat well, sleep well, and for a week forget about business.

The plane banked round, levelled out and descended to the runway. No matter how much flying he did, and it was a lot, Hunter always got a buzz out of it. Maybe he should have been a pilot but career decisions were a long time in the past, instead he just enjoyed the journey. He watched the flaps of the aircraft move, he saw the ground suddenly become close then felt the impact of the landing and the power of the engines as the pilot switched them to reverse thrust. How many landings had he made this year? Maybe fifty maybe more, this was a good one. As the aircraft slowed and started to taxi the other passengers burst into a round of applause. "Tourists." Thought Hunter, feeling slightly smug with his greater experience of and casual attitude toward flying.

When the plane reached the stand there was an almighty scramble for the overhead lockers leaving the majority of passengers standing uncomfortably packed in the aisle. Hunter stayed put looked out of the window and smiled to himself thinking, "What was the hurry? They would all be in the baggage reclaim well before their bags arrived." Eventually the doors opened and the passengers gradually disgorged down the aircraft steps and across the tarmac to a waiting bus. As they left most thanked the cabin crew who replied with fixed smiles as they would do again another three times that day. Once the queue for the doors had thinned to a trickle Hunter stood up and took a shoulder bag from the overhead locker then made his way unhindered to the aircraft door. Hunter was one of the last off, stepping into the warming morning air he already felt like he was on holiday, he slipped on a pair of sunglasses, tortoise shell Rayban Wayfarers, with green lenses, and sauntered to the airport bus where the rest of the passengers waited packed together hot and uncomfortable. Hunter stepped on, the doors closed and starting with a jerk that caused several over laden passengers to loose their balance, avoiding falling merely due to the fact that they were so closely packed together, the bus took them one hundred metres to the terminal. "Why do we have to get on a bus just to go so short a distance?" Hunter thought as the doors opened and he stepped off the bus and into the terminal. By being last off the plane he was first to passport control.

At the control point, a small booth with a window at the front and a hatch to the side, a uniformed official gave his passport a cursory glance and was about to stamp it when he paused and again looked up, he indicated to Hunter that he should take off his sunglasses, which he did, and looked at him more closely. Hunter was just over six feet tall, slim but well built, his thick black hair cut short but smart. He was lightly tanned which gave his blue eyes a more piercing quality, he was a good-looking man, but he was not vain. The face that looked back at him in the mirror was just his face, he was just built the way he was, he took care of his appearance and tried to keep fit, despite the hours he worked and time he spent travelling, but he didn't preen. The official looked Hunter up and down, from his sensible brown shoes, via his slacks and loose fitting white shirt to his face. Hunter smiled, the official did not. Instead he looked over into the baggage reclaim area. Hunter thought the official might have been looking for instructions but he could not see through. He couldn't envisage a problem, Greece is part of the Schengen Agreement and as a U.S. citizen he could visit for ninety days without a visa, so he waited.

In the baggage reclaim Maria stood casually to one side with a view of the passport control and the passengers coming through. She was a beautiful Mediterranean woman, olive skinned with wide dark eyes, her long black hair cascading over her shoulders. She was casually dressed, jeans and a blouse that was fitted better to show her exceptional figure. She saw the official look in her direction and acknowledged him with a nod.

The official turned back to Hunter. "I see you do a lot of travelling?" He stated but in the way of a question, his English competent but heavily accented.

Hunter relaxed, "Yes I travel a lot on business."

"And what is the purpose of your visit to Rhodes?" The official asked.

"I'm on vacation."

"Where are you staying?"

"At the hotel Bristol in Rhodes town."

The official thought for a moment as if he was trying to memorise this information then nodded, stamped Hunter's passport and handed it back.

"Thank you." Said Hunter, a hint of sarcasm in his voice. He slipped his passport into his bag and walked through to the baggage reclaim. There were only two carousels, one of which was slowly moving, carrying a single suitcase on a seemingly endless rotation that took it out of sight through a flap only to re-emerge a few seconds later from another flap.

Hunter stood by the second carousel, right next to the chute where the bags would come from. Normally he travelled light, just hand luggage, but he was on vacation so had brought more than normal. As the other passengers came through passport control they jostled around the carousel until it was packed three deep, those toward the back looking over the shoulders of those in front standing on tip toe trying to see if their bags were coming.

Meanwhile, unseen by Hunter, the passport official had left his post and joined Maria; they had had a brief conversation and left together.

Eventually the bags began to come up from the unloading bay and drop one by one on to the carousel. The passengers whose bags came first grabbed them excitedly complementing each other on the good luck of getting them first. Others at the back saw their bags go past but couldn't reach them through the

---

throng, some chasing them around the carousel but unable to get to them. After a while Hunter's bag dropped out, a simple grip, he picked it up and headed for the exit. He passed through the green channel, which was devoid of officials, straight through the terminal and out to the taxi rank where a queue waited impatiently for the next car.

Hunter cursed himself, normally he would have a pre booked car and driver waiting for him, but that was business, this was a vacation and he had not bothered. There was no meeting to get to, no rush, so he took his place at the back of the queue and waited, failing to notice that to the side and behind him Maria and the passport official were watching him from an idling white Mercedes saloon.

Hunter impatiently looked at his watch, an Omega Speedmaster Apollo, and cursed to himself, this was his vacation time, his own time and he didn't want to waste it in a taxi queue with a bunch of gabbling tourists.

The line of people moved slowly and he had been waiting for half an hour by the time he got to the head of the queue and wasn't in the mood for the old banger passing as a taxi that stopped to pick him up. Reluctantly he got in and was greeted by Greek music blaring from the radio, he gave the driver his instructions and was thrown back in the seat as the driver floored the accelerator and shot away from the rank while at a discreet distance, and unseen by Hunter, the white Mercedes followed.

The windows of the taxi were open and Hunter welcomed the cooling breeze, "just take it easy, after all you've been in worse taxis with worse drivers," he thought chuckling inwardly as he recalled a roller coaster ride through Istanbul in a nineteen fifties Chevrolet. Compared with that journey, this one was like a chauffeured limo ride into Manhattan. He looked out of the window and took in the landscape, which was so far uninspiring except the sea, which glimpsed between modern hotels looked so inviting. They passed an ancient looking old house and when Hunter turned to look at it again he saw the white Mercedes following them but did not register anything unusual about it. Then something struck him and he looked around again, "wasn't that the passport official" he thought but immediately the thought disappeared as at that moment the taxi pulled off the road and up to the Hotel Bristol stopping in front of the entrance. Hunter paid the taxi driver and grabbing his bags walked through the heat into the air-conditioned lobby of the hotel and approached the check in desk.

The waiting receptionist greeted Hunter with a "Good morning sir," and a welcoming if slightly false smile.

"Good morning," Hunter replied, "I'm John Hunter, I have a reservation."

The receptionist looked down at his computer and typed in a few letters, he then looked up again at Hunter, "Yes sir, we have put you in room 530 with a sea view."

"Good" said Hunter.

"If you would just complete this registration form please." The receptionist asked, passing the form and the pen across the desk.

Hunter took the form, briskly filled it in, and returned it to the receptionist who looked it over and typed some details into his computer. A machine whirred and the receptionist pulled out a plastic card, carefully placing it in a small specially designed envelope before handing it to Hunter. "Your key card sir. The lifts are over there" The receptionist gestured and Hunter looked in the direction indicated. "Would you like assistance with your luggage, sir?"

"No thank you I can manage." Hunter replied and taking his card turned and walked to the lift.

As Hunter waited at the lift Maria and the passport official came into the hotel. They saw Hunter waiting by the lift doors and quickly turned to look at a display of local produce for sale from the hotel.

The lift came down and the doors opened. Hunter stood to the side and let a couple of tourists out before he stepped in. As the doors closed Maria moved quickly over to the lift and pushed the button to call it back to the lobby while the passport official started briskly up the stairs.

Hunter stood alone in the lift and watched the lights indicate the passing of the floors. There was a ping and the lift stopped with the light indicating five.

In the lobby Maria had her mobile phone held to her ear. She saw the indicator panel light up five and simply said "Five." before ringing off and sticking the phone into the back pocket of her jeans.

The lift doors opened and Hunter walked out into a corridor that could have been in any hotel in any town. He looked at a sign indicating the direction of the rooms and turned left down the corridor checking the numbers on the rooms until he got to 530.

At the end of the corridor the passport official, breathing heavily, came through the doors from the stair well, immediately stepping back out of sight to surreptitiously watch Hunter go into his room. Once the door was closed the official broke cover and walked briskly down the corridor. As he passed Hunter's room he glanced momentarily at the door making a mental note of the number before turning back to the stairs and descending to the lobby.

In his room, Hunter dropped his key card on to the bedside table, dropped his bags on the floor at the end of the bed and went to the sliding glass doors that opened onto a balcony and a view of the sea. He slid the doors open and walked onto the balcony. Below was a terrace with tables and chairs laid out ready for lunch, a swimming pool where people were sunbathing, or swimming and beyond a sparsely populated sandy beach with a dark azure sea, glistening wavelets throwing up bright flashes of sun and in the distance the hazy outline of the Turkish coast. Hunter felt himself start to relax. This was what he needed, "If I spend the whole week just sitting here looking at this view it'll be ok." He thought to himself.

Outside the hotel Maria and the passport official got back into their car. Maria took out her phone pressed a button and waited for it to be answered. "Yes, he's in the Hotel Bristol, room five thirty. Yes we'll be waiting."

Coming in from the balcony Hunter looked around the room. It was pretty standard, double bed to one side a chest of drawers opposite with a small television on top and a mirror on the wall above that. There were small tables on either side of the bed with a lamp above each and a telephone on one. By the window there was a writing desk and chair and another more comfortable chair in the opposite corner. There was a short corridor to the entrance door with a wardrobe on one side and on the other a door leading to the bathroom. Hunter went into the bathroom, it was clean and white, white towels on the rail, a wrapped packet of soap on the sink along with small bottles of shampoo and body cream.

Hunter returned to the main part of the room picked up his bags and put them on the bed. He unzipped his grip and was starting to unpack his cloths when there was a knock on the door. He stopped what he was doing thought, "who could that be?" then went to the door opened it and was immediately knocked back into the room as three men burst in, two of them grabbed an arm each and pulled them tight up his back, the third, the passport official from the airport who had changed out of his uniform, pushed Hunter back into the room. "What the hell's going on!" Hunter shouted as he struggled but it was useless, he couldn't free himself and the men ignored his outburst.

As they pushed Hunter into the centre of the room Maria entered followed by Marcos, an older distinguished looking man with a full head of white hair and a neatly trimmed beard, which was predominantly white but still contained strands of darker hairs framing a deeply tanned face. He wore a lightweight grey suit and crisp white open neck shirt. Maria waited by the now closed door while Marcos walked into the centre of the room, looked around taking in his surroundings then turned to address Hunter. "So you thought you could come here without us finding you? You Americans are so naive."

Hunter was confused. "What do you mean?" he asked.

Marcos smiled to himself and chuckled. "Very good, very good," he said, then more seriously, "you know exactly what I mean."

"No, I do not know what you mean, I haven't got a clue what you're talking about, why you've burst in here... what the hell do you think you're doing?" Hunter replied angrily as he unsuccessfully attempted to wrestle his arms free again.

"I wouldn't expect you to admit it but you must have known we would be looking out for you and that if you came here, we would find you? What surprises me is that you were so bold and so soon." Marcos continued.

"You must be out of your mind, let me go this instant!" Hunter shouted.

Marcos stopped smiling, shook his head then indicated to the passport official who immediately punched Hunter hard in the stomach. Hunter doubled up gasping for breath. "Now stop wasting my time!" Marcos barked but stopped short, as there was another knock at the door.

Marcos turned to face Maria who shrugged then backed into the room. "All right open it, but don't try anything. Whoever it is get rid of them." Marcos ordered Hunter indicating the door.

Hunter felt the grip on his arms released. He took a deep breath and tried to stand up straight. His mind was racing. "What was going on? Who were these people?" Whoever was at the door knocked again. Hunter approached the door as the two men who had been holding him ducked into the bathroom and the others moved out of sight of the entrance. Hunter slowly turned the door handle and was greeted by a maid holding out fresh towels.

"Fresh towels?" She started to ask but before she had finished Hunter had grabbed her arms pulled her into the room and was running down the corridor.

The maid fell to the floor with a scream, her position blocking Hunter's assailants as they bundled out of the room in pursuit, the momentary delay giving Hunter a head start. He ran past the lift and into the stair well. Down he went helter skelter.

Maria took the maid into the room while Marcos called the lift and the others pursued Hunter down the stairs. At moments they could glimpse Hunter several floors below but couldn't get closer. Within seconds he had reached the ground floor and burst out of the stairwell into the hotel lobby, he looked around but the lobby was deserted, "what should I do?" he thought. Only one answer came to him, "Run!" so he ran, out through the hotel entrance and down the street. He didn't know where he was going, he didn't really know where he was, his instincts told him he must get away from his pursuers and to do that he had to move, and he had to move right then. As he ran he tried to formulate a plan, he would try to find a police station but he didn't know where there was one and he didn't have time to stop and ask, so he kept running. A few hundred metres from the hotel there was a dip and a bend in the road and Hunter was just out of sight when his pursuers came out of the hotel. One went left and one right both running in pursuit. Shortly afterwards Marcos and the passport official came out of the hotel, made to their car and drove off.

Hunter reached a side road and turned into it. He stopped, breathing heavily, and glanced back around the corner. He couldn't see anyone behind him, he looked again and saw the man who was chasing after him, so he took a deep breath and started to run again. He took another turn into a short road that ended on a main road on the other side of which were the walls of Rhodes old town. He had intended to explore the old town but he hadn't intended to do so so soon after his arrival, he had planned a leisurely morning strolling around, it had not been in his plans to be sprinting, trying to avoid, well he knew not who but that was the way it was going to happen. He crossed the road avoiding the traffic and ran down a flight of steps into the old dry moat then slowed to a brisk walk, trying to catch his breath, regularly glancing over his shoulder hoping he had now given his pursuer the slip.

The two men who were chasing after him met at the steps and paused, looking around trying to get a sight of Hunter. Spotting him they jogged down into the moat and followed gaining ground but trying to stay out of sight.

Hunter had got his breath back and was beginning to think he had evaded his assailants when glancing back he saw them several hundred metres behind, tracking him. He quickened his pace trying to act is if he hadn't seen the men following him, all the time looking for an opportunity to escape.

The town walls were tall, solid and unbroken. To his left above the moat ran the road. "Maybe I should go that way?" but as he thought that he saw a white Mercedes cruise slowly past. It rang a bell in his mind and he recalled having seen it as he had arrived at the hotel, he remembered his impression that the passport official had been in the car, and then he realised that the man who had punched him in the stomach was also the man who had checked his passport at the airport. He felt he was on the edge of a revelation but couldn't quite piece it all together as he was more concentrated on his escape. "Which way to go?" he thought. He picked up his pace and then the opportunity he had been waiting for arrived, a flight of steps leading up to a tunnel in the walls. Without a backward glance he suddenly turned and ran up the steps into the tunnel.

Hunter's pursuers saw him go, one started running after him while the other pulled out his mobile phone and pressed a button, waiting a few moments for an answer, before speaking. "He's in the old town, we'll try to head him toward the harbour". He nodded as he listened to the response then pressed another button and started to run after his accomplice.

Hunter came out the far end of the tunnel into the old town of Rhodes and found himself on a busy street thronging with tourists, it was ideal. Hunter quickly mingled in slowing his pace to the speed of the crowd, pausing and looking into shop windows as the group around him did so. He tried not to look back and be recognised but he felt compelled to and in so doing he saw his pursuers. He thought they hadn't seen him but he ducked into a souvenir shop to make sure.

The shop was packed with gaudy local ceramics, racks of T-shirts with Day-Glo lettering, posters depicting scenes from the island, sunglasses, flip flops, inflatables of all shapes and sizes and a cornucopia of tat that the owner thought would appeal to holiday makers. There were a few shoppers idly looking at the goods on sale watched by an old woman who sat behind a counter by the door, her beady eyes silently following the customers as they disinterestedly picked up then returned items from and to the shelves. Hunter stood to one side behind a rack of T-shirts and sun hats, but in sight of the entrance. He flicked through the T-shirts feigning interest while looking out for his pursuers. He felt the gaze of the shopkeeper turned to her and smiled, there was no reaction. He returned to his watch and seeing the men walk past he ducked down behind the rail. The shopkeeper raised herself up and looked down at him, he looked up at her, smiled again and still bent down waddled around the rail. Then inspiration hit him, he pulled a garish T-shirt off the rail, grabbed a broad brimmed sun hat and took the biggest pair of sunglasses from their rack.

"No, women's." Said the shopkeeper.

Hunter now standing up but keeping his back to the door ignored the shopkeeper and passed her a large bill. While she counted out the change, he took his shirt off and pulled on the T-shirt, all the while keeping a sideways watch on the door. He put on the hat and sunglasses, put his own sunglasses in his trouser pocket tied his own shirt around his waist and walked out leaving the shopkeeper waving a handful of small notes in his direction. He had gone, so she shrugged and with a smile put the notes in her own purse.

Hunter walked back in the direction he had come from, the streets were busy, shopkeepers trying to entice the tourists in with a wave and the offer of the best price possible. Hunter tried as hard as possible to be unobtrusive, he certainly looked different, but the further he went the more he thought he might have overdone it. No one else was quite as badly dressed, and he felt he stood out even more than before. He moved slowly with the flow, keeping his head down but behind his sunglasses looking in all directions.

Hunter rounded a corner and bumped straight into another man. He looked up apologising and in an agonising moment recognised the man as the passport official from the airport, the man who had punched him in the stomach, He was not so quick to recognise Hunter who instantly turned back round the corner and moved off quickly through the crowd. It took several seconds for the official to realise who Hunter was, his disguise had worked, before after a double take he headed after Hunter talking into his mobile phone, giving Hunter's new description. He saw Hunter ahead and shouted, "Stop, thief, stop him." Hunter started running, pushing his way past people, the crowd opening for the official who kept shouting "stop him!" but fortunately for Hunter he was surrounded by tourists who not only couldn't understand Greek but either had no intention of getting involved or were too involved in their own relaxation to notice. Hunter turned a corner into a narrower busier street, and despite trying to barge people out of his way his progress was slowed and he found it impossible to gain any sort of lead on the official who was slowly catching him. The crowd thinned and Hunter was able to run again. He turned the first corner he came to and almost ran straight into a flower stall, a trestle table on the pavement covered with buckets filled with flowers. In an instant he grabbed the table and pulled it over, the flowers falling onto the road forming a multicoloured carpet, the buckets in which they had stood rolling around their water flowing into the gutter, the stall itself half blocking the road. The official rounded the corner at a run, he half hit the turned over flower stall then his feet went from under him skidding on the slippery mass of flowers and water, depositing him hard on his backside. He tried to get up slipped again then got to his feet, he looked around but in vain, Hunter was out of sight.

Hunter did not look back but instead turned into an archway he paused looking around and saw a deeply recessed alcove which he went into, trying to make himself as small as possible as he pushed himself against the cold stone wall in the darkest corner at the back. He tried to control his breathing and waited, not daring to look out in case he was spotted.

Unheard by Hunter, the official was talking on his mobile phone as he walked slowly up the street. "I almost had him, I think he's gone through the arch... yes in your direction...ok I'll follow, he should come straight toward you."

Hunter was about to duck out of his alcove when glancing out he saw the official turn into the archway. Hunter stepped back unseen into his corner and again tried to make himself as small as possible. The official walked straight past the alcove without looking in and Hunter exhaled with relief, without realising it he had been involuntarily holding his breath, although it was only seconds it felt like minutes had passed since he'd last breathed and he took in great lungfuls all the time trying to stay as quiet as possible. He tried to calm himself, tried to come up with a plan. First he ditched the hat, then pulled off the T-shirt turned it inside out and put it back on, finally he took off the cheap sunglasses and put his Raybans back on. He didn't look much different but the change might buy him a few seconds. He paused a little longer then ducked back out of the arch in the direction he had come from. This time he strolled casually through the passers by, he didn't know where he was or where he was going, he was following his nose and his nose lead him into the main square.

The square was bathed in dazzling sunlight and all around it's edge were restaurants, their terraces shaded by awnings and giant parasols. Some people were finishing lunch, others were sitting in the sun enjoying a drink watching the world pass by. Each restaurant had a man standing outside, a 'caller in' pestering passers by to come in, have a drink, have a meal, all of them had the best food, the best prices. Most people ignored them, as Hunter did, walking around the edge of the square trying to stay anonymous but he wasn't paying attention and suddenly found himself accosted by one of the restauranteurs.

"Hello my friend, you look very thirsty, come in and have a lovely cool drink." He said.

"No thank you." Hunter replied trying to continue past the man who blocked his way.

"But we have the best cocktails, fresh juices, a cold lager maybe? A glass of wine?"

Hunter tried to side step him but the restaurateur was persistent, they danced from one side to the other the restaurateur gesturing toward his establishment.

"I said no!" Hunter shouted straight into the man's face. Realising he was defeated the restaurateur stood to one side but as he did so Hunter saw one of the men from the hotel standing at the end of the square looking at the faces of tourists. Hunter turned back to the restaurateur. "You persuaded me."

The restaurateur was delighted. "Yes sir, you have made a good choice, please I have a nice table for you right at the front here, you will have a lovely view of the square."

"No I want to sit at the back." Hunter demanded.

The restaurateur was surprised, "Of course sir where ever you want."

Hunter followed the restaurateur into the cool shade, and on to the back of the terrace. "There." Hunter pointed to a table behind a large group of men.

"But you will not be able to see..."

Hunter cut him short. "There!" He barked.

The restaurateur gave in. "Of course sir as you wish." He showed Hunter to the table. Hunter sat down and immediately picked up a huge drinks menu and holding it up in front of his face peered over the top and between the heads of the men in front. He scanned the square, then realised that the restaurateur was hovering, waiting for his order. "Beer!" Hunter ordered continuing to look out on the square. The man left him and Hunter continued to look out. He could see the one man waiting, watching, who was shortly joined by the official who had been chasing him. They talked animatedly and pointed first in one direction then the other. "What are they planning?" Hunter thought.

A long cold lager was brought to Hunter's table, the waiter slipping a till receipt under the glass then looking in the same direction as Hunter fascinated to know what was so interesting. All he could see was the square thronging with tourists. He shrugged and turned to take an order from another table. Hunter, his beer untouched, continued to watch the men in the square and saw one of them take a call on his mobile phone. There was a short conversation before he put the phone back in his pocket. A conversation with his colleague followed and they both looked in Hunter's direction. Hunter sank lower in his chair covered from sight by the men in front.

The men in the square started to walk down the line of restaurants looking closely in each one until they were in front of the restaurant where Hunter was trying to remain out of sight. At that moment the men in front stood up to leave. This was Hunter's opportunity, he stood up behind them and followed as they moved out toward the square, but the subterfuge was not enough, he was too obvious and he was spotted by the passport official. Hunter saw the man's expression of recognition and as he pulled his colleague's sleeve pointing to Hunter he bolted, hurdling the row of tables at the front of the restaurant catching one with his trailing leg knocking it flying, glasses of drinks smashing on the ground. He crashed straight into the restaurateur, who was chatting to some young women at the front of the restaurant, knocking him straight into them. The restaurateur tried to stop himself falling and in doing so grabbed one of the girls' bikini tops pulling it down. The girl screamed, covered herself with one arm and with the other slapped the restaurateur hard around the face.

Hunter sprinted across the square, the crowds parting to let him through, the two men in hot pursuit, he had a lead, but not much. He ran back through the arch and on the other side took the risk of glancing back behind him. The men had gone. Hunter was surprised but relieved. He slowed down to a brisk walk and in moments found himself in the open looking out over the harbour. He looked around and could see no sign of his pursuers but failed to notice the white Mercedes, parked a short distance away, or who was inside, if he had done he might have made haste.

Along the quayside was a row of tourist boats moored stern to, sunlight reflecting from the water along their white hulls. One of the boats, engines running, was loading with passengers, an orderly queue making their way up the gangplank and finding seats either in the sun or under the shade of an awning at the stern of the boat.

Hunter stopped a short distance away and looked out over the water toward the harbour entrance. "I'm supposed to be on vacation," he thought to himself and gazed out to sea trying to make sense of what had happened since he'd arrived that morning. In his reverie he failed to see Marcos and Maria get out of the car and approach him.

"So you thought you could get away from us?" Marcos said.

Hunter looked up, his train of thought broken.

"Come on Johnson, you know Rhodes is a small island and we know every inch of it. You cannot escape us. So you may as well come with us now and stop this ridiculous chase." Marcos continued.

"Johnson?" Hunter interrupted, "I'm not Johnson, you've made a big mistake."

"Johnson, Smith, Jones, you can call yourself whatever you want. I know you as Johnson and Johnson you shall be. You were a fool to come here and even more foolish to try to escape from us. Now, we're wasting time, are you going to come quietly or do we have to use force?"

Hunter looked around and saw the other men, who had been chasing him, closing around.

"I'm not Johnson and I'm not coming with you!" Hunter said defiantly.

Marcos shrugged and snapped his fingers. His accomplices closed in around Hunter, he was trapped his back to the water, his mind feverishly attempting to find a route of escape. He looked around and saw the gangplank of the tourist boat being pulled up. That was it, that was his chance. Hunter waited until the first man was within reach grabbed him, span him around and pushed him off the quay into the water. Then he ran toward the tourist boat which had cast off it's mooring and was starting to move away from the quay. As Hunter reached it, without breaking pace, he leapt, just managing to catch the boat's railing as it gathered pace. One of his pursuers leapt after him but was too late, missing the boat completely and falling face first into the boats churning wake.

Marcos, Maria and the official stopped short on the quayside then turned away, leaving their accomplices who were floundering in the water to rescue themselves.

Hunter hung for a moment and watched them leave then with the help of a small group of passengers pulled himself up and over the railing onto the boat.

"You must have really wanted to come on this trip." Said one of the passengers.

"You don't know how much." A panting Hunter replied with a smile.

A sailor pushed his way through the group that was gathered around Hunter. "That was a stupid thing to do." The sailor said. "Are you alright?"

"Yes, thanks."

"You still have to pay." The sailor said then reached out his hand. "Fifteen Euro."

Hunter reached into his pocket, and pulled out some notes. "Where are we going?" Hunter asked as the sailor took the money.

"Down to Lindos and back." The sailor replied giving Hunter a ticket.

"How long does that take?"

"About an hour and a half each way. We stay close to the coast but we don't stop." The sailor replied. "Enjoy the journey." With which he turned and left.

The group that had gathered around Hunter had dispersed, taking their seats or standing by the rail looking out at the town or watching the wake of the boat as it cut through the dark blue harbour waters. Hunter turned to lean against the rail and watch the buildings of the town recede as the boat made its way out through the sea walls. He thought about what had happened to him that morning. "Who was Johnson?" "What did these people want from him?" More to the point, "why did they think that he, Hunter was Johnson?" Now he had time to decide what to do. The obvious thing was to go straight to the police. He had seen enough of these people to give a good description, for all he knew the police might know who they were. Then he would know whether he could stay and have the vacation he'd promised himself, or get off the island and head back home. He had three hours on the boat so he could at least relax for that time. All of a sudden he felt very tired, very hungry and very thirsty. He turned away from the rail and walked along the deck to a doorway that led into the saloon of the boat. There were a few passengers in the saloon, some sitting looking out through the large windows the others buying cold drinks or a snack, so he didn't have to wait long to get served. The choice was limited but it was enough. He got a lemon Fanta, a large black coffee and two bread rolls, filled with tuna fish and salad. He picked a table where he could see out and sat down. He gulped down the Fanta and hungrily ate the first of his rolls, then sipped his coffee, it was strong, just as he liked it. He took longer to eat the second roll savouring the coffee as he did so. When he had finished he returned the coffee cup to the counter bought another and went back outside immediately enjoying the cooling effect of the sea breeze. He looked out over the rail at the rocky coast where he could spot the odd angler or sunbather who had found quiet spots away from the populous beaches. After a short while he walked across to the seaward side where the breeze was stronger. There he looked out to the horizon where the white sails of a distant yacht, that was just in view, reflected the sun and stood out clearly in the clear bright air. From the corner of his eye he noticed a sleek fast power boat someway to the stern,he looked out again at the distant yacht then turned his attention back to the powerboat. There was something about it that made him want to look again more closely, it seemed to be tracking the tourist boat, keeping a steady distance behind. Near to Hunter a passenger was watching the sailing boat through a pair of binoculars. Hunter approached him.

"Could I just borrow your binoculars for a moment" Hunter asked.

The man did not speak English, so Hunter gestured to the binoculars and with a shrug the man passed them over. Hunter pointed them toward the powerboat and turned the focusing ring until the view was clear. There on the boat were the easily recognisable figures of Marcos and Maria. Hunter passed the binoculars back to the tourist with a "thanks." and made his way back into the saloon where he sat down with his back to the stern of the boat trying to keep out of sight, and wondering what the next move would be.

Opposite him an older lady sat looking out the rear facing windows in the opposite direction to Hunter. She looked over to him, "Don't you want to see the view?" She asked.

"I just need to cool down, I had to run for the boat." Hunter replied.

"I don't know why, they run every hour." She said.

"I've got an appointment to keep, in Lindos." Said Hunter.

The lady nodded, seemingly satisfied and looked past Hunter out of the window. Then a thought crossed her mind. "If you've got an appointment why didn't you go by car? It's faster." She asked.

Hunter could have done without the interrogation but the lady was only being friendly, "I had time and I enjoy going by boat. At least I thought I had time, that's why I had to run to catch this one." He answered.

The woman looked Hunter up and down. It made him feel uncomfortable, then he realised he had his T-shirt on inside out, this time he ignored her and glanced over his shoulder. He couldn't quite see the powerboat but he sensed that they would still be following. The older lady continued to watch Hunter as he stretched his neck to see over the heads of the passengers sitting outside. The powerboat was still there, keeping pace with the tourist boat. The old lady half stood up to see what Hunter was looking at and as Hunter turned back she immediately sat down realising that he had caught her, then after a pause asked, "are they friends of yours?"

"Who?"

"The people on that speedboat."

"Not really."

"Are they following you." She asked excitedly.

"No." Replied Hunter, the tone of his voice revealing that he was lying.

"Is it a chase? Are you a wanted man?" She asked.

"No and No." Hunter answered firmly indicating that the conversation was over. He turned his chair so that his back was toward her and looked out the window.

The lady seemed to lose interest, but kept half an eye on Hunter who every now and then half stood up to check the position of the boat. After a short time he could no longer see it. He felt flustered, "Where had they gone?" he thought. "They know

I'm on this boat." He stood up and went to the windows on the seaward side of the saloon and saw the powerboat cruise past then pick up speed and power away. Hunter sat down again and let out a sigh of relief.

"So they aren't after you?" The lady asked.

Hunter turned and smiled at her, "As I said no, I don't know who they are."

The lady returned Hunter's smile and relaxed into her chair to enjoy the journey. Hunter sat down, but was almost immediately on his feet again as the boat started to slow.

"We're just going into a bay." The lady said. "Why don't you come outside and get a proper view, I believe it's very pretty?" She got up and waited for Hunter who followed her out. They stood together by the railing and as the boat turned a headland they were greeted with a view of the bay.

It was just what Hunter had hoped for when he booked his trip to Rhodes. The bay was open, the sides flanked by white limestone cliffs, high rocks that dropped straight into deep water which were topped by a thin cover of trees and shrubs. At the land ward end a stony beach dotted with sun-beds, most occupied, other bathers, who could or would not pay lying on towels, swimming, or just paddling. The beach was backed with white rocks, a line of steps winding up through them to a small cafe shaded by pine trees. The water of the bay darkened from the turquoise blue of the shallow water to the aquamarine of the deep and around the edges Hunter could pick out the odd snorkel. There were a few pleasure boats a little way off the beach and among them, stationary but engines running, the powerboat that had been following him. Hunter tensed then jumped, as the ships' horn sounded unexpectedly and loudly just above him, then to cover his obvious nervousness, he dropped down to a crouch pretending to tie his shoelace.

The powerboat was blocking the path of the tourist boat so the captain waving from the bridge gave another long blast on the horn. The powerboat moved slowly out of the way around to the opposite side of the boat from where Hunter hid.

"So they are following you!" The old lady said triumphantly from above him.

Hunter looked up to a friendly face and smiled almost laughing. "Let's just say there's someone on that boat I'd rather not talk to at the moment."

The tourist boat turned so that Hunter's side faced the beach and all the passengers moved over to that side surrounding Hunter, taking photos of the beach talking excitedly, providing Hunter with further cover.

"Can you see the powerboat?" Hunter asked the lady.

"No it must be on the other side, wait, hold on, it's just coming around." She looked down but Hunter was gone.

Hunter staying in a crouch had made his way through the passengers and quickly through the saloon to the seaward side of the boat. It was time to get off and back to land. He climbed over the railing and lowered himself down so that he was hanging from the edge of the boat then he let go and dropped into the water. It was colder than he expected and as he surfaced he suppressed a yell, he took a quick look around then swam round to the bow of the boat that was now almost stationary giving the passengers an opportunity to take in the view and take their photographs. Hunter trod water and waited, he looked around the land ward side of the boat and saw the powerboat coming toward him, He took a deep breath, dived down under the water and started to swim strongly toward the shore while behind him the tourist boat started to pick up speed and turned back out to sea. Hunter was unaware of this but despite his need to surface for breath he kept going, he didn't want to brake the surface where he could be seen out in the open water so he swam on, lungs bursting until he reached a chain. Looking up he could see it was anchoring a large buoy so he followed the chain to the surface broke through and took a huge lung full of air. For a while he stayed low in the water breathing heavily, then making sure he was hidden by the buoy he looked around to seaward and saw the tourist boat leaving the bay, the powerboat following. He hung onto the buoy and watched as the powerboat accelerated throwing up a great white wake and powering out to sea. He breathed a sigh of relief, for the moment he felt safe.

CHAPTER 2

On the beach Kate Adams had been disturbed from her book by the sound of the ships horn. She had sat up on her sunlounger and watched as the powerboat had circled around the tourist boat, it's crew appearing to be looking for someone, she was no expert on nautical matters but to her it seemed strange. She had sat up taller and looked more closely over the top of her sunglasses when she thought she had seen a man's head in the water close to the bow of the boat which then disappeared, maybe she'd been mistaken, but she continued to scan the bay as the tourist boat started to move away, and then she saw someone pop up by the buoys in the middle of the bay, she couldn't be sure from that distance but there was something about the way he seemed to be hiding behind the buoy, furtively looking out after the departing tourist boat, that spurred her interest.

Hunter suddenly felt something hit him on the head. He tensed inside and turned to see a beach ball floating next to him, a group of bathers waving and shouting for him to throw it back. He threw the ball in the air and hit it volleyball style back to them then pushed away from the buoy toward the beach. Keeping as low in the water as possible he mixed with the other swimmers before swimming into the beach.

Kate watched him come in and laughed openly when he stood up, his waterlogged cloths hanging off him. Hunter shook himself then pulled off the T-shirt wringing the water out. Kate noticed his well muscled lightly tanned body, and followed him with her eyes as he walked up the beach directly toward her. As

Hunter came close Kate said, "Do you always swim with your cloths on."

Hunter stopped in his tracks and noticed Kate for the first time. As he looked over, what he saw was a shock of long blonde hair, framing a tanned face which accentuated her even bright smile, her white bikini only served to highlight her slender but feminine figure and long shapely legs. His day had suddenly got a whole lot better. "Only when I'm feeling modest." He replied with a smile.

Kate picked up and held out a towel. "Here have this."

"Thanks." Hunter replied moving closer and taking the towel. He sat down on an empty sunbed next to Kate and dried himself off, he took off his shoes and socks, which he wrung out and laid on the sunbed to dry, then stood up again and unselfconsciously took off his trousers, he gave them a shake before hanging them off the back of the sunbed, leaving him in just a pair of black Calvin Klein boxers. Kate watched his every move, and when he caught her looking she turned away and blushed slightly. Hunter passed the towel back. "Thanks." He said.

"You're welcome," Kate replied, "I always keep a spare, just in case a fully dressed man comes out the sea."

Hunter smiled at her with a grimace and sat down again.

"Anyway, what were you doing out there fully clothed? I didn't see you going in." Kate asked.

Hunter thought quickly, "I was scrambling along the rocks around the headland and slipped in."

Kate looked at him disbelievingly, then shrugged and looked out at the bay. After a few moments she turned back to Hunter and with a great sweeping gesture toward the bay said, "Leonis bay is very beautiful don't you think."

"Yes it's very picturesque." Hunter replied.

Kate almost leapt off her sun-bed with excitement. "As I thought, you don't even know where you are. This is Anthony Quinn bay."

Hunter tried to play it cool. "Is it, I wouldn't know I only flew in today."

Kate had the bit between her teeth. "Come on Mr...What is your name anyway."

"Hunter."

"Well Mr Hunter, do you know what I think." Kate continued.

Hunter shrugged and lay down on the sun-bed. "I'm sure you'll tell me."

"I think you jumped off that tourist boat and then swam in here." Kate phrased her statement in the way of a question and accusation.

Hunter shrugged again, "Why would I do that?"

"So you don't deny it?"

"I do deny it, but I'm fascinated to hear the rest of your theory."

"That's the problem, I don't know why you would jump off the boat.... though it might be something to do with that powerboat that was circling around, they seemed to be looking for someone. Are you being chased?"

Hunter laughed, "I think you're a beautiful girl but with an over active imagination, looking for a holiday adventure." He said pointing at her book, a trashy thriller.

Kate put the book down embarrassed.

"Thank you for the compliment, but I'm not on vacation, I live on the island." She replied assertively.

"Really? I'm sorry I just assumed, why are you living here?" He asked.

"I'm studying for my doctorate, and it's about certain aspects of the development of Greek civilisation, so I thought I should live where it happened, at least while I'm researching.".

"Working hard today?" He joked.

Kate smiled and gestured with her head towards some strapping Greek men lying on the beach working on their tans. "Just studying the Greek architecture."

Hunter laughed, and they both lay back on their respective

sun-beds, then Hunter sat up again. "Do you have a cigarette?" He asked.

"No. It's bad for your health."

"You're quite right I haven't had one for a while but somehow I feel I need one."

"The cafe up the path will sell them."

Hunter grabbed his damp trousers and felt in the pockets. He pulled out one damp and disintegrating note. "They're not going to take this." He said to Kate.

"I shouldn't encourage you." Kate said and relenting reached into her beach bag and pulled out a note offering it to Hunter.

"Are you sure?" He asked

Kate nodded "Sure, but are you sure?"

There was a beat, Hunter wasn't sure, he had never been a heavy smoker but even so, giving up had been one of the hardest things he had done.

Hunter took the money. "Sorry I know it's a dirty habit but I've had a kind of rough day."

"You can get me a coffee while you're there."

"How do you have it." He asked.

"Black." She replied.

With that, Hunter slipped his shoes back on and headed up the path to the cafe which was really a wooden shack with a shutter facing the bay that opened up to form a counter. In front were plastic tables and chairs with umbrellas to shield the customers from the sun. Some were occupied by locals or tourists in their swimming costumes, some talking, others just taking in the sun and the view, which from there was even better. Pop music played from speakers hung from the cafe roof, it was a relaxed happy scene. Hunter would have liked to enjoy it but he couldn't relax until he knew who was chasing him and why. Hunter ordered two coffees and bought a pack of cigarettes and a lighter. He lit up while the coffee was being prepared and stood admiring the view. The nicotine hit his blood stream and his legs went a little wobbly. He cursed himself, he knew that once an addict always an addict and this one cigarette would lead him back down the path to become a smoker again but after the day he had had he needed it. It was a prop but at the same time it felt great. The coffees were put on the counter so Hunter stubbed out the cigarette, paid, picked up the plastic cups and carefully carried them down to the beach.

While Hunter was at the cafe Kate had been busy. She wanted to know who this strange man was, a man who came out of the sea fully clothed but claimed it was an accident. A man who seemed in no hurry to go anywhere. Once Hunter was out of sight she went through his pockets but found only his Raybans. She replaced the trousers where they had been and looked at his T-shirt. Unlike the sunglasses it was the cheapest nastiest tourist T-shirt she had seen, which didn't fit its rather urbane looking owner at all. She replaced the T-shirt and lay back down on her sun-bed unsure what to make of the situation.

When Hunter returned Kate was where he had left her reading

her book. He gave her her coffee and the change from the bill she had given him. He sat down again sipped the coffee, it was good and strong, then lit another cigarette. He lay back and started to relax.

Kate looked over at him. "I can't keep calling you Mr Hunter, what's your first name?" She asked.

"John," Hunter replied, "and yours?"

"Kate, Kate Adams."

"It suits you very well."

"Thanks, I'm kind of used to it."

There was a pause as they both drank their coffee. Hunter could sense that Kate was building up to another question. She turned to him again. "Come on John, I've bought you a coffee and cigarettes, tell me truthfully what were you doing in the water fully clothed?"

"I thought we'd dealt with that." He replied a hint of irritation in his voice. He turned and looked at her. "Can you take off your sunglasses please."

Kate lifted her sunglasses to the top of her head pulling her hair back off her face and Hunter looked straight into her sparkling blue eyes. The intensity of his gaze made Kate feel uncomfortable but she could tell he was trying to make a decision, she felt a tingle of excitement, what was he going to tell her.

Indeed Hunter was trying to decide, could he trust this girl. She seemed perfectly pleasant, normal, trustworthy and although he was looking in her eyes his peripheral vision was taking in the rest of her body. He couldn't deny it, she was a good-looking girl and he was a sucker for a good-looking girl. He made his decision.

"Can I trust you?" He asked.

Kate was a little taken aback, this sounded serious, maybe she didn't want to know, after all she didn't know this man, he could be involved in anything. "You don't know me." She answered.

"Exactly, and you don't know me."

Now Kate had a decision to make. She could get up and leave, forget all about it, never see this man again, or she could just get involved in something she didn't want to. On the other hand it may be something completely innocent. Whatever way, her curiosity was getting the better of her, she wanted to hear the story, beside which there was something about this man she liked, his good looks for sure but there was something more, a solid quality, a self assurance that stopped short of over confidence or arrogance and above that there was something intangible that made her trust him.

"Yes you can trust me, I'm good with secrets." She said eventually.

"I don't have a secret," Hunter replied, "just a problem, and I'm not sure I want to involve you. In fact I haven't got a clue how I got involved. You're sure you want to hear?"

Kate nodded.

"I'll give you the edited highlights for now. You know I only arrived on the island this morning," he looked at his watch, "About four hours ago, and was planning a very relaxed day. Check out Rhodes town, a good lunch, a dip in the pool, a bit of sun, cocktails, you get the picture." He took out another cigarette and lit up, taking a deep drag. "Well I had just got to my hotel room,"

"Which hotel?" Kate interrupted.

"The Bristol." Hunter replied.

"I know it." Kate said.

"Anyway," Hunter continued. "As soon as I'd got in the room a bunch of tough guys burst in and grabbed me."

Kate laughed. "Come on now you're winding me up!"

Hunter shook his head. "Honestly, it sounds ridiculous and far fetched but it actually happened, to me as I say just a few hours ago."

Kate whistled "You are telling me the truth?"

Hunter nodded, "Yes I am."

"How many of them were there?" She asked.

"Well there were three and they caught me totally by surprise, obviously, so I couldn't do anything about it. Then their boss came in, an older guy, and some woman, good looking but with an evil look in her eye. The funny thing is I think one of the three guys was a passport official from the airport."

"Are you sure?" She asked.

"Fairly, not a hundred percent, but... anyway, I managed to get away, then they chased me through the town to the harbour where they caught me again."

"What happened then."

"I managed to get away and jumped on the tourist boat, then I saw they were following me in that powerboat. So I slipped over the side and the rest you know."

"That's incredible." Kate was astonished. "Why were they after you?"

"I haven't got a clue. The funny thing is when they caught me at the harbour the boss kept saying I shouldn't have come back and called me Johnson."

"Johnson? I thought your name was Hunter?"

"It is, they must have mistaken me for this Johnson character."

"It's quite a story."

"I know, I don't get it myself. Well I think I do, they think I'm Johnson and this Johnson has done something they don't like, or got something they want, to be honest I don't care, I just want them off my back."

"Go back to the beginning and tell me the whole story, in detail."

So Hunter recounted the whole story in as much detail as he could remember and as he did so it sounded even more fantastic. He wouldn't have believed it himself if it hadn't happened to him and he was surprised that Kate didn't tell him to push off there and then. When he had finished there was a pause as Kate thought and Hunter lit another cigarette.

"What are you going to do?" She eventually asked.

"I don't know, I don't think I can go back to the hotel, I would imagine that they'll be waiting there, so I've got no passport, no money, no phone," He looked at the T-shirt, "and no clothes."

"The obvious thing is to go to the police. I've got a car up there," Kate pointed toward the cafe as she spoke, "come on we'll get it sorted out in no time."

"You're right I should go to the police, are you sure you want to drive me, I don't want to inconvenience you?"

"It's fine, it's only twenty minutes in the car, anyway I'm not sure how you'd get there otherwise, there's no bus from here."

"In that case I'll be happy to accept, but I'll tell you what,"

"What?"

"I'm knackered, do you mind if we stay here for a while, I could do with a rest, get my head in order before I see the police."

"Yes alright, I'm going to have a swim, but then we'll go straight there."

Hunter watched her walk down the beach and slip into the water, and thought, "well maybe some good will come out of this," then he lay back closed his eyes and was asleep within seconds.

When he woke, the beach was in shadow, the low evening light describing the detail of the surrounding rocks. The colours of the sea were richer, the sky a darker shade of blue, it was what photographers call magic hour, where all the colours are richer, the shadows darker and more extensive. There were few people on the beach now, a couple of swimmers and just one boat moored in the bay rocking gently on the slight swell. Some fishermen had set up on the rocks at the entrance of the bay their rods sticking out like thin antennae. Hunter looked toward Kate who had slipped a halter neck dress over her bikini and was looking out toward the sea. She noticed Hunter was awake and smiled at him.

"Do you feel better?" She asked.

Hunter nodded. "Yes thanks." He sat up lit a cigarette and looked at his watch. "I've been asleep for four hours?"

"M hum. Sleeping like a baby. I didn't have the heart to wake you."

"I'm sorry to keep you here all that time."

"No it's fine I always like to stay 'till the evening, it's the best part of the day. Incidentally your clothes are behind those rocks." She said pointing behind them "that boat came back so I hid them, I don't think they spotted you."

Hunter sat up suddenly fully awake. "What did they do?"

"Don't worry, I saw them come 'round the headland, so I bundled up your things and covered you with a towel then as they came into the bay I sat on your sun-bed and pretended I was talking to you."

"I'm surprised that didn't wake me up, what happened then?"

"They just cruised around for a bit, then went off again."

"You're sure they didn't see anything?"

"Pretty sure."

"Ok we'd better get a move on, I should get back to town and see the police as soon as possible."

"I'm ready when you are."

Hunter got up found his now dry clothes, pulled on his trousers and T-shirt then sat back on the sun-bed to put on his shoes. Kate slipped on her sandals, picked up her large shoulder bag and stood waiting for him. They made their way up the path past the cafe where the chairs were now full, the customers catching the evening sun, enjoying a cold beer. The smell of barbecuing fish filled the air.

"Incidentally, when we've sorted this out I'd like to take you for a really good meal." Hunter said to Kate, "You've been very kind."

"Thanks, I know some great places, I'll enjoy that." She replied.

Behind the cafe a level area served as a rough car park. Kate led Hunter to a dusty slightly dented orange Renault Twingo. She rummaged in her bag for a moment before producing the car keys, opened the passenger door for Hunter then got in and started the engine. "I don't normally have any dealings with the police so I'm not a hundred percent sure where to go, I know I've seen a Police station in Rhodes town, and I'm pretty sure I can find that one."

"Fine, hopefully we'll get it sorted and then I can get back to the hotel."

Kate drove out the car park and up a bumpy track that passed through fields of olive trees to the main road. They turned right onto the main road and within minutes were passing through Faliaraki, the main resort for package holidaymakers. The main street was lined with bars restaurants and night-clubs, the sidewalks packed with people who, although Hunter didn't know it, were mostly British. Hunter was amused by their demeanour strolling around in vests and flip flops, their skin sunburnt and the majority sporting cheap tattoos of one sort or another. He smiled outwardly but inwardly made a deal with himself, that he would never come to a place like this.

Kate saw him smiling, "What's so funny?"

"Nothing really, but these people, I've never seen so much sunburn or so many tattoos."

Kate laughed, "Are we a bit of a snob Mr Hunter."

"I guess I must be."

Kate laughed, "Don't worry we'll be in town soon."

Fifteen minutes later they were entering Rhodes town.

"I think the police station is this way." Said Kate, turning onto the inner ring road.

They drove around the town for a short while before the road ran past a section of the city walls.

"I recognise that." Said Hunter pointing to the walls. "I had a very quick tour this morning."

They continued into the new town centre. Kate turned off the main road and made several turns before she pulled up in a quiet side street. "I'm sorry I thought I knew where it was but I was wrong. I'll have to ask." She got out of the car and stopped a passer by. Hunter watched from the car as a conversation ensued which looked more like an argument, there was much arm waving and pointing before he saw Kate nod then return to the car. "Ok I wasn't far off we'll be there in a minute," she said as she got back in. The police station turned out to be just a few streets away and soon they were parked outside. "Shall I come in with you?" she asked, "You may want some help in case they don't speak English."

"Thanks, but I think it might be better if you don't, "I think it might be better if you weren't involved any further."

"I'll wait here then, I want to know the outcome."

"I could be a while."

"I've got my book, besides you owe me a dinner"

Hunter didn't want to push it any further, he didn't really want her to leave, in fact he hoped things would be quickly sorted out and he could start his vacation again, this time by having dinner with Kate.

"Ok you can hold me to that." With which he got out of the car.

"Good luck." Kate shouted after him.

He gave her a wave and went into the police station.

The lobby of the police station was starkly lit with fluorescent strip lights, the walls were painted a drab light green and adorned with posters, mainly in Greek, some in English and German warning tourists about pickpockets. There was a wooden bench and opposite a counter behind which sat a bored looking sergeant. Hunter approached the sergeant.

"Do you speak English?" Hunter asked.

"A little." The sergeant replied,

"I need your help," Hunter continued. "A gang of people tried to kidnap me this morning and have been following me ever since. I think it's mistaken identity."

The sergeant looked a little blank, "wait here," he said, then got up opened a door behind him and had a brief conversation in Greek. He was followed back to the counter by a young police officer, the Sergeant took his seat again and the young officer addressed Hunter

"I speak English, tell me what is the problem."

"It's quite a long story," Hunter replied is there somewhere we can sit down.

The police officer looked Hunter over, "Ok come with me." He opened a flap in the counter and a door beneath allowing Hunter to follow him behind the counter and into the back room. The room was decorated in the same way as the lobby, the wall opposite containing a securely barred window. Filing cabinets lined one wall and there was a sofa against the other. Against the wall where he had come in, Hunter saw that there was a table with a coffee machine and a packet of cellophane wrapped sandwiches which he assumed must be the officer's evening meal. There was a fridge in one corner and in the centre of the room four desks, a chair on either side, and to Hunter's surprise on one of the desks a gun belt. The officer sat behind this desk, put the gun belt in a drawer and motioned for Hunter to sit down, which he did.

"Tell me the story."

"It's all very strange, I wouldn't believe it myself if it hadn't happened to me," Hunter started, "I only arrived here this morning..."

Hunter told the young officer, who took notes and occasionally interrupted with detailed questions, the whole story. When he had finished, the officer looked at him somewhat disbelievingly, "This is quite a story, but there are certain elements that tie in to other things I've heard today, I'm sure it is all a mistake and you have nothing to worry about, but we will investigate. I'll need to speak to this Kate Adams, but I can do that at your hotel, I'll come back there with you now." With which he got up took the gun belt out of the desk and put it on. Hunter followed him out through the waiting area, the police officer pausing to have a brief conversation with the sergeant.

Outside, Hunter led the police officer to where Kate was parked and opened the passenger door. "This officer wants to talk to you but he'd like to do it at the hotel, will you drive us 'round there?"

"Sure, get in."

Hunter squeezed into the back while the officer sat in the front passenger seat for the short drive to the hotel. No one talked on the journey and once they were there Kate pulled up in a parking space at the front and they went in.

In the reception the police officer stopped "would you mind waiting over there?" He asked Kate gesturing to a seat on the opposite side of the lobby from the reception desk. Kate did as she was asked while the officer accompanied by Hunter approached the reception desk. The officer addressed the receptionist in English so that Hunter could understand. "Do you recognise this man?"

"No." The receptionist replied.

"He claims to have checked in here this morning." The officer stated.

"Ah, I do the night shift," Replied the receptionist, "What is the gentleman's name."

"Hunter, John Hunter," Hunter interrupted, "room five thirty."

The receptionist looked through the register. "Ah yes Mr Hunter we do have you down as being in room five thirty. Is there a problem?"

Hunter went to speak but the police officer held up his hand to stop him. "Was there an incident here this morning?"

"Not that I know of, of course the daytime receptionist would know more than me."

"What about the maid?" Hunter interrupted.

The Police officer looked at him with displeasure. "Mr Hunter please do not interrupt," Then to the receptionist, "When will the day receptionist be here?"

"Seven tomorrow morning," The receptionist replied.

"And when do your chamber maids start?" The police officer continued.

"At the same time. Could you tell me what this is all about?" The receptionist asked.

"No, I will speak to them in the morning. Now, I'd like to speak to the manager please."

"I'll call him, but I'm afraid again the night manager is now on duty."

The police officer thought for a moment, "would you ask him to come here and wait for me," he turned to Hunter. "in the meantime I'd like to look around your room please."

"Yeah sure," Hunter replied, then to the receptionist, "Could I have a key card please, I think I left mine in the room."

The receptionist took a plastic card placed it in a machine, pressed a button then pulled it out and handed it to Hunter. "There you are sir." He said.

With a "thanks," Hunter and the Police Officer turned and went to the elevator. They waited for a few moments for the lift which when it arrived was empty. Nothing was said on the way up and to Hunter's room.

When Hunter entered the room, everything was as he had left it. He looked through his bags to check but everything was there, wallet, credit cards, mobile phone, clothes, all was in place. "Everything's there," He said turning to the Police Officer who nodded then took a cursory look around the room and in the bathroom.

"I'm going to speak to Miss Adams and the manager now but apart from that there's nothing I can do tonight."

"But these guys might come back."

"I doubt it, the officer replied, anyway what do you want me to do? I don't know who these people are and there is nothing to go on apart from what you have told me, besides I don't have the resources to do anything more. Keep your door locked and I'll see you in the morning." With that he turned and left.

Once the door was closed Hunter stripped off went into the bathroom and had a quick wash. He put on clean clothes, put his wallet and mobile in his pockets, and was about to leave the room when he stopped and thought again, he took a lightweight blue Harrington jacket out of his bag, then left.

Back down in reception Kate was talking to the police officer. She saw Hunter come out of the lift, glance at her, indicate with an expression, then go through to the hotel bar.

The police officer had first asked Kate about herself then about what had happened that afternoon. She had described events from her point of view and asked a few questions of her own which went unanswered. Then the police officer asked some more direct questions about how well she knew Hunter and why she was involving herself, she had blushed slightly then, and given a half answer, masking the truth.

"Be careful Miss Adams, you don't know this man, I don't know why he has made up this fantastical story but honestly I don't believe a word of it. I suggest you go home, and keep away from him. Meanwhile I will carry out some checks and I'll be in touch in due course." With that he got up and returned to the reception where the manager was waiting to speak to him.

Kate was now in a quandary, she wasn't sure whether to follow the police officers advice. Was she being naive? A man comes out of the sea fully clothed with an incredible story, she should probably run a mile but she had an investigative mind and needed to find out the truth for herself.

When Kate came into the bar she saw Hunter sitting on a stool leaning on the bar sipping a beer. She sat down next to him and looked straight ahead.

Hunter could see that she was in a quandary.

"It is true." She asked and looked around at him.

Hunter smiled, "Yes it's true."

Whether it was his calm expression or the way he said the words Kate believed him. "Thank you, the policeman sowed a seed of doubt, but I do believe you."

"I'm glad someone does." Hunter replied, a note of frustration in his voice.

"Everything Ok?" Kate asked.

Hunter stared straight ahead, his brow furrowed

"Not really, the police obviously don't believe a word of it, that officer almost told me as much, I'm pretty furious, I mean why would I want to make up a story like that? What possible reason could I have? So now I'm left here to fend for myself against, well I don't know who, or why. I've a good mind to just pack up go to the airport and get the next flight out of here."

If Kate still had doubts they evaporated. If this was an act, it deserved an Emmy. She could see that Hunter was genuine and genuinely worried. "Why don't you?" she asked.

"Why don't I what?"

"Get the next flight out of here?"

Hunter looked around at Kate his face now set firm. "Because I don't like to be pushed around and...I want to find out what's going on."

"Shouldn't you leave that to the police?"

Hunter smiled a conspiratorial smile. "I should, but they're not going to do anything."

There was a pause as they both thought, then Hunter continued. "Ah, what am I talking about? It's been a difficult day, I'm not going to do anything, you're right I should leave it to the police and they're probably right, mistaken identity, the thing that bothers me is that they just don't seem to take it seriously and what worries me...is...well I feel exposed. They came here once so it's the obvious place for them to come again that is if there isn't someone here already watching me."

"What are you going to do then?"

"I suppose I should book into another hotel get a good nights sleep and see how things look in the morning."

"You seriously think they might come back?"

"Yes, they seemed pretty pissed off with this Johnson guy, I don't suppose they're going to give up that easily."

Kate thought, "Well, if you want you can stay at my place for the night. It's so hidden away no one will find you there."

Hunter was taken aback. "Are you sure? I mean you hardly know me."

"It's just one night, I'll take the risk. Make your mind up before I change mine."

"Thanks, I accept. Just one thing I've got to be here for the police in the morning."

"I'll bring you back I have to come into town, let's go straight away just incase you are right."

Hunter necked down his beer then they got up and made their way straight out to the car.

As they drove away from the hotel a man watched unseen in the shadows, he noted down the number of the car then got out his mobile phone and made a call.

Soon they were out of Rhodes Town and heading south on the coast road, past the airport and through small brightly-lit coastal towns, the shops still open, the streets thronging with tourists. After half an hour they left the last of the towns as the road climbed uphill, the full moon reflecting the light of the sunken sun across the dark water. They turned off the main road and headed inland before turning up a dirt track which ended in front of a small white single story house. Kate turned off the engine and got out, Hunter followed as Kate walked up to the house.

"Aren't you going to lock it?" He asked.

Kate laughed looking back over her shoulder as she opened the front door. "There's no need, no one even knows this place is here, apart from the farmer who rented it to me, splendid isolation, it's great for studying, no distractions."

Hunter followed her into a modest room, earth red tiled floor, white walls, the ceiling formed by the inside of the roof. There was an open plan kitchenette with a breakfast bar at one end, a fireplace at the other and opposite the front door French windows. Next to the kitchenette was another door which lead to the bedroom. Next to the fireplace was a sofa a pile of books to one side and a rug on the floor.

"Nice place." Hunter opined.

"It's big enough for one. Sit down, I expect you'd like a drink."

"You read my mind."

"What will you have?" Asked Kate opening a kitchen cabinet.

Hunter sat down on the sofa. "Have you got a gin and tonic, large one?"

"I think I could manage that."

"Oh, and have one yourself!" Hunter said jokingly.

"Thanks, I may just do that."

Kate made the drinks and Hunter picked up the top book from the pile. It was about the history of Rhodes, he flicked it open then put it down again, it was in Greek.

Kate brought the drinks over handed one to Hunter and sat down cross-legged on the rug.

"It's all Greek to me," He said holding up the book, "Thanks," holding up the gin and tonic.

"Very funny," Kate replied, "Cheers." She reached forward and they clinked their glasses. "You can see I do study."

Hunter took a good drink, "That feels better," He said. Then felt a craving for another cigarette, he got to his feet.

"Where are you going?" Kate asked.

"I need to smoke." Hunter replied.

"We can sit outside if you like."

"Yes that would be good."

Kate went over to the kitchenette and got a saucer. " Here use this I haven't got an ashtray." She said passing the saucer to Hunter. Then they went out through the French doors and sat down on a couple of plastic chairs. Hunter lit up and watched the smoke in the moonlight as he blew it vertically upwards into the night sky. A moment passed as they sipped their drinks, then Kate looked over at Hunter. "Come on then tell me a bit about yourself, so far all I know is that you're a man who comes out the sea fully dressed, claims to have been chased by a bunch of villains, then somehow gets a poor innocent student to drive him around and take him into her home. By the way that shirt is better than that awful T-shirt you were wearing before."

"Thank you, I didn't spend a lot of time choosing The T-shirt you know, it was supposed to be camouflage." He paused as Kate laughed. "I'm afraid I'm not that exciting really. I'm from Montana, went to business school, qualified as a lawyer and now work in corporate finance. I came here for a vacation, but so far it's turned out to be anything but, anyway what about you, what's your story?"

"I'm from Missouri, both my parents are college lecturers so I guess I was always destined for academia, as I said that's why I'm here working on my PhD thesis."

"You're very lucky, from what I've seen so far it's a beautiful island."

"Yes it is but most of the time I've got my head in books or I'm writing. Today was a bit of an exception I don't normally take a whole day off."

"Good for me that you did. I'd have been pretty stuck without you."

"I think you were right when you said I was looking for an adventure, I love my subject but..." She trailed off without finishing her sentence then her mood seemed to change, "You must be hungry, I know I am, would you like something to eat?"

"Yeah, that would be great."

They got up and went inside. Hunter sat down and lent back on the sofa while Kate went over to the kitchenette opened the fridge and looked in. "I can make an omelette and salad." She said over her shoulder, there was no reply from Hunter, he was fast asleep on the sofa. Kate smiled closed the fridge and went through to the bedroom.

CHAPTER 3

When Kate got up Hunter was still asleep on the sofa, the night before she had covered him with a blanket but otherwise left him as he was. He looked as if he hadn't moved all night. The whole room was filled with sunlight and through the windows Kate could see that as usual the sky was cloud free and bright blue. Kate filled the kettle and put it on the stove, then got out a cafetière and two cups. When the kettle had boiled she made a strong brew of coffee, poured out the two cups and took one over to Hunter. She paused for a moment, then gently shook him.

"Wake up sleepy." She said.

Hunter stirred under the blanket, but his eyes didn't open. Kate shook him again more vigorously and this time Hunter opened his eyes then immediately closed them. "It's so bright." He said.

"Welcome to Rhodes," Kate answered, "Come on I've made you some coffee."

Hunter opened one eye and reached out a hand taking the coffee cup from Kate. "Thanks." He murmured. He sat up straight and took a sip of the coffee. "That's good, what happened last night?"

"You fell asleep, so I went to bed."

"Oh, sorry,"

"It's fine you must have been exhausted."

"I was,"

"How do you feel now?"

"Tired, sleepy."

"I'll sort that out, come on, on your feet." Kate pulled the blanket off Hunter, then took the coffee cup from him.

"What's going on?" He asked.

Kate held out her hand, which Hunter took, and pulled him to his feet. "Take your shirt and trousers off!" She ordered.

"Come on Kate, it's a bit early for games surely." But he could see from her expression that she wasn't messing about so complied with her instructions.

"Now hold my hand and close your eyes."

Hunter complied again, taking her hand as she lead him out through the French doors into the garden. He smelt the fragrance of the plants and felt the warmth of the morning sun on his shoulders, and then within an instant he was falling and a split second later he was immersed in the cold water of the swimming pool, the shock of which brought his senses instantly back to life. He broke the surface, spluttering but wide-awake to see Kate above him laughing. In an instant he grabbed her ankle and pulled hard. Kate lost her balance and with a yelp was in the water with him. She came to the surface face to face with a grinning Hunter.

"I guess I deserved that." She said, dived down and did two lengths underwater then started to climb out. Her soaking dress clung to her like a translucent second skin and Hunter couldn't help himself stare.

Kate caught him looking and splashed water into his face. "Mr Hunter!" She said feigning indignation. Then turned and went back into the house. Hunter swam a couple of lengths then pulled himself out of the pool and lay drying out in the sun.

Kate re-emerged in a towelling beach robe, a towel over her shoulder carrying a tray on which were the two cups of coffee, Hunter's cigarettes and a lighter. She put the tray down and sat next to Hunter, and passed him the towel.

"Thanks." He said reaching over and taking a cigarette. He inhaled deeply. "That's good." He said, then pausing, "In fact it's all good."

Kate looked at him quizzically, "What do you mean?" She asked.

"The sun, the sky, the coffee, the cigarette....you."

Kate blushed turned and went back into the house, "I'll fix some breakfast." She said over her shoulder.

Hunter looked at the pool, the water returning to its glassy unruffled state. "Fool," he thought, "That was so ham fisted, why can't you just be cool and keep your mouth shut." He lay back and closed his eyes soaking in the sun's revitalising energy his mind wandering, recalling the image of Kate coming out the pool. He must remember that moment, the images of our lives fade unless we make a conscious effort to hold onto them, no mater what happened this was one he wanted to hold onto. The warmth of the sun made him drowsy and he had entered that half state of sleep and wakening when Kate called from the house. "Come on it's ready."

When Hunter went into the house he found the breakfast bar set out with two places, fresh fruit in a bowl, bread, cereal, milk, a board with a selection of cheeses and a pot of fresh coffee.

"This looks great," He said, "I feel pretty hungry."

"I'm not surprised," Kate said, "We didn't have anything last night, if you remember, help yourself."

Hunter pulled on his shirt and trousers then sat down and started breakfast.

When they had finished Hunter excused himself, went outside and lit up another cigarette. Kate followed him. "I'm sorry to spoil the holiday atmosphere but shouldn't we be getting back to see the police?"

"You're right of course," Hunter replied, "Let me freshen up and we can get going."

He finished his cigarette and followed Kate in.

Hunter was ready and waiting when Kate came out from her bedroom dressed in jeans and a T-shirt. "Come on then." she said picking up her bag and opening the front door. Hunter followed her out to the car.

In the light Hunter was able to see the lane they had come down and when they reached the road he looked back. Sure enough the house couldn't be seen. "Quite a nice hideaway," He thought as Kate turned out onto the road.

They didn't talk much on the journey into town, Kate pointed out the sights and told Hunter the names of the villages as they passed through, while Hunter just made polite acknowledgement. He was thinking about what the police would say and what the consequences would be. Soon they were back at the hotel, Kate pulled up but left the engine running, "Aren't you coming in?" Hunter asked.

"No I've got work to do."

"Will I see you later?"

"I'm not sure I've got a lot to do, but I'll call you."

"But you haven't got my number."

"I'll call the hotel."

"Ok."

There was an awkward pause and Hunter started to open the door then Kate looked up and smiled, "Good luck, I'm sure it will all get sorted and I will call later." Then impulsively she lent forward and kissed Hunter on the cheek. "Go on you're late already."

Hunter got out of the car and went into the hotel. Kate stayed and watched him go in. Once he was out of sight she went to put the car in gear at which moment there was a knock on the side of the car which startled her, making her jump. A man in a suit was leaning over looking in at her.

"Pardon me miss, I need to have a word with you." With this he showed her a Police identity card. Kate was taken aback but she nodded her consent.

When Hunter entered the hotel lobby he was greeted by the Police officer from the previous night. He was not happy. "Mr Hunter, where have you been? I've been waiting for you."

"I'm sorry," Hunter replied, "I didn't feel comfortable here so I stayed with a friend."

"The girl? Miss Adams?"

"Yes that's right."

"How well do you know this girl?"

"I only met her yesterday."

The police officer thought for a moment, then looked at Hunter with a knowing smile. "I understand. Now I have spoken to the receptionist who remembers you checking in but does not remember you running out of the hotel, I have spoken to the chambermaid who said that she hadn't seen you, the manager knows nothing either."

Hunter went to interrupt but was cut short by the police officer.

"I've checked at the harbour and the found a sailor who saw

you jump onto the boat, but he couldn't say if you were being chased or not. It was a foolish thing to do, now I don't know whether you are some sort of fantasist but I don't believe a word of this story."

Again Hunter tried to speak but the police officer ignored him and continued.

"If you want to try to impress a young woman with some story that's up to you but do not waste police time doing it, you are lucky I don't charge you, but really I can't be bothered with the paperwork. Enjoy your holiday, enjoy Miss Adams company but do not bother us again!" With which he turned on his heels and left. Hunter was dumbstruck. What could he do now? He hadn't made the story up, he didn't know who the men were or whether they would come back again. His one helper, Kate, had disappeared and although he thought he could probably find her place again he wasn't sure that he would be welcomed. He needed to think.

His room was as he had left it. He opened the patio doors and went out onto the balcony. He sat down and lit up a cigarette paced for a moment then sat down deep in thought. He put his feet up on the edge of the balcony rail and lent back trying to blow smoke rings. His mind wandered back to when he was a kid. He had always enjoyed it when after lunch his father lit up a cigar, and with little persuasion from Hunter, would blow smoke rings for his amusement. Now whenever Hunter smelt the distinct aroma of cigar smoke it reminded him of his childhood. His father had been a reticent man with a dry sense of humour, he was kind but even then Hunter could sense that there was something that held his father back emotionally. Hunter knew that he had been in Vietnam but he never spoke about it, even though as a child Hunter had been fascinated to know what daddy had done in that war. With age and experience Hunter now believed that it was his wartime experiences that held his father back from outward displays of emotion. What terrible things had he seen, what terrible things had he done, how many of his friends had been killed? Hunter never knew and had learned never to ask.

The other overriding quality Hunter remembered about his father was that he was totally reliable. Someone to look up to, who if he arrived somewhere would immediately be in command of the situation, a big man. Hunter knew he was not his father but as he thought about him realised that now was the time that he too needed to man up and take control of the situation. The Police wouldn't be there to save him and he was buggered if he was going to let these guys give him the run around. But what could one man, with no experience of these matters do against a gang of, he assumed, hardened criminals?

As he pondered his next move his mind in a world far removed from its present place the phone rang. Hunter's train of thought was broken and he did that thing of for a moment trying to work out who could be calling him rather than actually answering the phone and finding out. He got up and went into the room lifted the receiver and said "Hello."

"John?" It was Kate's voice at the other end of the line.

"Hi, Kate, I'm sorry I was out on the balcony thinking."

"That's ok, I'm sorry I had to rush off there were just things I needed to do. How did it go with the Police?"

"Rubbish, they think I'm a fantasist and nothing actually happened, I'll get no help from them, anyway I'll tell you all about that when I see you, that is if I am going to see you?"

"Yes that's what I was calling for, I've got a lot to do but I can see you this evening."

"Great where?"

"Well have you ever been to a Son et Lumière?"

"No what's that?"

"It's a sound and light show, there is one on the edge of the old town, just near your hotel, they'll be able to give you directions. Just meet me there at nine."

"Ok will you have had dinner?"

"Probably not."

"Then I'll take you out afterwards."

"Ok. The Son et Lumière at nine."

"Got it."

"See you then. Bye"

The phone went dead leaving Hunter with more to think about. Kate's voice hadn't sounded quite the same, tenser he thought and the conversation seemed a little abrupt. He also thought that the Son et Lumière was a strange place to meet. He went back onto the balcony leant on the railing, looked out at the sea and rationalised. She must just be busy and tired, besides she'd only met him yesterday and she couldn't be sure that he was telling the truth or just as the police thought a fantasist. The Son et Lumière was a perfectly good place to meet, why not? As he looked out at the peaceful happy scene he started to wonder himself. What was the truth? Had he imagined it? Had he over reacted to something? He had been under a lot of stress, a lot of travelling, and boy did he need the rest. He snapped himself out of that train of thought, of course it had really happened, he wasn't stupid, he didn't make things up. The real question was what would happen next? Or would anything happen? Maybe they had realised he wasn't Johnson and would leave him alone. He decided not to worry about it any longer, he could go crazy turning it over again and again in his mind. Instead he went back into the room got a beer out the fridge and a book out of his bag then went back to the balcony and settled down for a relaxed day of sun and reading. If anything happened it happened and he would deal with it then, in the meantime he'd loose himself in his book.

That evening Hunter felt good, nothing unusual had happened to disturb his relaxation. No strange men had burst into his room and no one had chased him through the town. He'd read for a while making inroads into his holiday book, an adventure novel hurriedly purchased when he had changed planes in London, had some lunch on the restaurant terrace and a swim in the afternoon. Now he was preparing for what he hoped was a date with Kate. He checked his watch, there was still plenty of time, so he headed down to the hotel bar and had a leisurely but rather strong gin and tonic before leaving to meet Kate.

The evening was sultry and warm and beyond the light

pollution of the town he could see the stars sparkling far out in space. He tried to recognise some constellations but soon gave up, he wasn't an amateur stargazer let alone an astronomer.

Light traffic passed by as he walked down to the old town and pretty soon found himself outside the Son et Lumire. There was a short queue of tourists at the ticket booth, so Hunter joined them and pretty soon had his ticket and was in. The Son et Lumière was a secluded railed off area of park between the road and old city walls. Lines of chairs were set out on the grass the border lined with palm trees and other typical Mediterranean bushes and plants. Hunter scanned the seats and, failing to see Kate, sat down on the near edge of one of the middle rows. Shortly afterwards the display started. Initially there was just music, a classical introduction building up to a crescendo then a pause before the music started again accompanied by a fantastic light display. Hunter was starting to become absorbed in the show when Kate arrived slipping onto the seat next to him. She shouted into Hunter's ear, "Sorry I'm late the parking was a nightmare." Hunter smiled his acknowledgement and nodded. A few more latecomers slipped into the seats behind them and unseen by Hunter, who was watching the display, Kate glanced nervously back at them.

The crowd were enjoying the show, oohing and aahing and applauding at particularly spectacular moments. Hunter had never been to such a show, and wouldn't have if Kate hadn't asked him, but he was thoroughly enjoying it. He glanced at Kate a broad grin on his face and catching his movement from the corner of her eye she looked round, "It's great, thanks." He said in a raised voice. Kate smiled nervously although Hunter didn't notice as his attention had turned back to the light display.

Then it went dark. A prolonged drum roll started and Hunter felt something stick in his back. He turned to ask whoever it was behind him to stop it and found himself face to face with one of the men who had broken into his room and chased him the day before. Hunter made to jump up but was pushed down from behind by another man.

"I wouldn't do that." The first man said straight into Hunter's ear, "It is, a gun." Hunter stayed still, the stale garlic smell of the mans breath lingering on his nostrils.

"Stand up slowly and head for the exit." The man said.

Hunter looked around at Kate who had stood up to let him out. His expression was imploring asking, "What's going on?"

Kate looked embarrassed, "they're police officers." She said quietly.

Hunter moved past her, the man close behind, the gun stuck into the small of Hunter's back. The second man followed as they headed for the exit. Kate watched and as Hunter glanced back his face saying "Why?" Kate was lit up with a spectacular flash from the restarting light display and he could see her expression was confused, almost apologetic.

Outside a car was waiting, there were plenty of people around and Hunter guessed this might be his best chance, he span around pushing the mans arm that was holding the gun away from him but as he did so, the second man had hold of him. Hunter's moment was gone as the two men bundled him into the back of the car, squeezed in themselves and shut the door as the car moved rapidly away.

Hunter had to stay cool, keep his wits about him, and wait for the opportunity of escape. He looked out the window, he wanted to know where they were going and what route they were taking he needed to remember every detail.

Once they were away from the city centre traffic the driver looked around, it was Maria. "Blindfold him."

The man closest to Hunter held him down by the shoulders as the other man tied a cloth around Hunter's eyes. He couldn't see now but he could still sense. Estimate the speed of the car, the time taken, remember any turns.

They had been heading out of town toward the coast road, up which he had travelled with Kate the night before, when he was blindfolded, so he assumed that was the way they were going. He tried to estimate the speed of the car and count the time, but the car slowed several times, as they went through the small towns. He could tell this from the sound of people on the streets and the penetrating bass of dance music as they passed the open doors of night-clubs and bars.

His mind turned to Kate, "why had she betrayed him? Why had she said they were the police? Had she been duped or was he a mug, and a big one, to trust her." He couldn't believe that. He didn't know Kate really but he always felt that he was a good judge of character and his judgement was that she was ok.

The car turned off the main road, "How long had it been?" Hunter tried to make a mental note. Then the car turned again seeming to go back on itself before turning again and proceeding along a winding road that felt as though it was going uphill, a feeling that was reinforced by the rising tone of the cars engine. They turned off this road and made many more changes of direction before eventually slowing to a halt. Maria turned off the engine and Hunter knew they had arrived. Hunter was completely confused, as far as he knew they could be at the far end of the island, back in Rhodes town or somewhere in-between. The door opened and the man next to Hunter pushed him out into the grip of another man who led him into a building. Their footsteps echoed on a tiled floor as Hunter was jostled along and into another room. The man stopped him and Hunter felt what he assumed was a chair pushed up against his legs, before a pressure on his shoulders indicated that he should sit down. A short time passed before the door opened and Hunter heard three sets of footsteps, one of them a woman's. He heard a chair being pulled back and caught the distinctive smell of cigar smoke, the smell that evoked his childhood, but he knew this was not a childhood game.

Something was said in Greek and Hunter felt his blindfold removed. He blinked in the bright electric light and managed to focus on a woman's stockinged leg. He followed it up to see Maria sitting on the edge of a desk. Her heavily made up lips open revealing a grinning set of bright white teeth. Behind the desk sat Marcos.

Hunter waited as Marcos sat back looking at him inhaling smoke from his cigar then blowing it up in the air. He put the cigar down on a large, brass, fish shaped ashtray and lent forward his elbows on the desk.

"You gave us the run around yesterday, I wasn't happy, but I have to admire your," The man broke off and looked up to the ceiling trying to find the right words, "Tenacity? Anyway that does not matter now, you made it easy for us with that girl, I'm surprised at you, you've always been so careful, it was out of character but no matter," he lent forward to add emphasis to his words, "where's the head?"

"What do you mean the head? I don't know anything about a head."

"Oh Johnson, please stop wasting my time."

"I'm not Johnson."

The man slammed his fist on the table. "I'm not going to waste my time with this nonsense, I don't know why you are making up this stupid story, it's me Marcos, I'm Marcos now and I've always been Marcos, you're Johnson and you always have been now tell me where the head is!"

"I don't know what you are talking about, I'm a tourist, John Hunter, I don't know who you are, I don't know anything about a head, I don't know why you think I'm Johnson, I'm just here on vacation, there's nothing more I can tell you!"

The man leant back in his chair again and laughed. The others laughed with him as if on queue. Then he leaned forward again. "You've come to trade, fine, if we were on the other side of the Atlantic, we'd have to trade, but we're not. I would say we hold the upper hand, so here's the deal. Give us the head and we put you on the next plane home, keep up this pretence and you stay on Rhodes, forever."

Hunter needed to think, he needed to buy time, there seemed little way out of the situation. "Look, if I was Johnson..."

Marcos interrupted, "What do you mean if? Stop wasting my time!"

Hunter spoke in a measured way, "Just hear me out, if I was Johnson, and I'm not, I'd be pretty foolish to come here wouldn't I. I'd know you'd be on the look out, that you know the island and would find me, so why would I do it. It doesn't make sense."

"I've never known how your mind works, and I don't really care, maybe you thought you were so clever you'd...I don't know...I just want the head."

"Well I haven't got it."

The man made a signal then leant back in his chair as one of the men held Hunter tightly against the chair. Maria leant forward from the desk so her face was close to Hunter's, she licked her lips then raised her arm. Hunter just caught a glimpse of something bright as she brought her arm down, he felt a blow and then dampness on his face. He looked up defiantly just as a second blow came down on his other cheek which also immediately felt damp. The woman threw her hair back revealing a smile of satisfaction then held up her hand to show Hunter a diamond ring, the stone cut to a point.

"Nothing?" Marcos asked.

Hunter looked back in defiance, lips held tight, the blood from the clean straight cuts on his cheeks running down his face.

The woman now had a small bottle with a dropper in her hand. She leaned forward. Hunter struggled, but the man holding him was too strong. The woman held the bottle in front of Hunter's face and drew some liquid into the dropper. Then she dropped some liquid onto the cut on Hunter's right cheek. The pain was searing, Hunter screamed and struggled but was held tight. The woman laughed and dropped some liquid into the cut on Hunter" left cheek. The intensity of the pain took Hunter's breath away, he screamed again, involuntarily, and was left head down panting. When he raised his head he wished he hadn't as the woman was waiting dragging her long fingernails, cut like talons down his left cheek and over his wounds. She laughed maniacally, she was obviously enjoying herself. "You bitch." Hunter mumbled, and regretted it as the woman first repeated the treatment on his right cheek then gave him two hard slaps.

Hunter braced himself for further treatment but it didn't come. He looked up.

"That's just a taste, Maria can be quite cruel you know and very inventive, I don't think you want me to leave you with her for the night, I just want the head, but even if you tell her she'll continue to use you for her enjoyment. It wouldn't be nice, so my advice would be to tell me where the head is now. It will save you a lot of pain."

Hunter's mind raced, he believed what Marcos was saying but didn't know what to do.

"I'm waiting." The man said.

Hunter was speechless, racking his brain for an exit, Marcos gave Maria a resigned look, and nodded, she smiled with pleasure but at that moment Hunter had an idea.

"Ok," he gasped, "Wait."

Maria looked around at Marcos, disappointment etched on her face.

"I've got the head, here on the island,"

Marcos looked interested. "I knew you hadn't got it away,"

"But obviously I haven't got it on me."

"So tell me, and the boys will go and get it."

"That won't work, I need to get it, but I need time and I need to be alone."

Marcos laughed. "You really do take me for a fool don't you?"

"No not at all," Hunter replied, "but neither am I. I had to take precautions just in case of this eventuality. Without me you'll never get the head, and if I'm not alone...anyway I'm sure you have your people watching the airport and the ports, so I can't get off the island, let me go and I'll contact you within twenty four hours to arrange the hand over."

The man laughed again, "oh dear, you are very funny, but why not? I can wait a day, and then Maria can have her fun, I expect in that time she'll come up with a few more ingenious ideas for her pleasure and your pain. On the other hand if, and it's a big if, you come up with the goods, I'll keep her off you."

Maria looked at him angrily, "They'll be others my dear, you'll have your fun." Marcos reassured her, then to Hunter "Right I'll let you go but you've got twenty four hours and if I don't have the head Maria will have....well not your head necessarily."

Maria purred with excitement at the prospect leant forward and kissed Hunter on the lips, he looked up disgust in his face, and in a fit of pique Maria went to slap him again, but the moment she raised her arm Marcos was on his feet, he grabbed Maria's arm and held it back.

"You'd better go, I can't always control her," He said to Hunter.

"I'm going I don't need a second invitation to get away from that psycho," Hunter said nodding in Maria's direction. Maria struggled to get at Hunter but Marcos held her back.

"How will I make contact with you?" Hunter asked.

Marcos thought for a moment, "Just go back to the hotel, we can find you there."

Hunter nodded stood up and turned to leave then paused, "Don't follow me." He warned.

Marcos shrugged, "of course not."

The two other men stopped Hunter at the door and put the blindfold back on. Hunter didn't resist, he had managed to escape from the situation, he would wait for them to drop him off, go to the hotel then straight to the airport and the first flight out. He would take the rest of his vacation safely at home and put his Rhodes experience down to exactly that, experience and a good although totally unbelievable story to tell over dinner.

One of the men opened the door then stopped when Marcos spoke. "Wait. Just remember this, if for some reason you manage to leave the island, Maria will pay a visit to your girlfriend, and Maria is even less sympathetic with women, I think it goes back to being bullied as a child, but I'm not a psychiatrist, needless to say it wouldn't be pleasant, for Miss Adams that is."

As he heard those words Hunter realised that he couldn't just duck out, "Keep her out of this," Hunter said trying to keep his face unemotional. "She knows nothing, is nothing, just a pick up."

Marcos laughed and waved his hand with which Hunter was pushed through the door. "So Kate wasn't involved with them, or was that a double bluff?" He was confused, "he had trusted Kate but she had betrayed him." Then he remembered the look on her face when the men had lead him away from the Son et Lumière. Something didn't fit, she had looked shocked and uncertain, maybe she had been tricked, he just couldn't believe that she would have set him up like that, he had got her involved, he couldn't just save himself and abandon her and from his recent experience he wouldn't want Kate to be left to the psychopathic Maria. He needed to see her and find out the truth.

Hunter was bundled outside and into the car. They headed off at high speed and again Hunter tried to memorise the route, the information may have come in useful, but it was just not possible to estimate the speed and distance or remember all the turns.

The car pulled up at the roadside and Hunter was pushed out. He pulled off the blindfold and saw the car speed off back in the direction it had come from. He took in his surroundings, there were no buildings just dry scrubland, the road heading straight in either direction along the coast, the sea dark, the moonlight reflecting on the water in a long line from the horizon to the shore. In the distance he could see the lights of a town tight on the coast. It was the opposite direction from which the car had gone so that was the direction in which he started to walk.

As he walked he felt the landscape become more familiar. He stopped and looked back in the direction from which he had come. He was sure he had seen that view before but it was difficult to tell in the dark. He walked on and after what he guessed was maybe another half mile came to a junction, this he did recognise so turned off and headed up the side road. Sure enough the road was familiar, he'd been there just that morning. He picked up the pace and was soon at the track that led to Kate's house. He paused, his previous misgivings playing on his mind, then decision made walked up the track.

When he got to the house he saw Kate's car outside and a sliver of light emanating from a crack in the front window shutter. He went to the front door and was about to knock but stopped in mid action. Instead he crept around the side of the house trying to make as little sound as possible. He could hear music through the walls and as he came up to the French windows he crouched down and took a quick careful glance through the glass, then more boldly a longer look. He couldn't see Kate fully, just her leg, as she was sitting on the sofa which was pushed up against the wall adjacent to the French windows. Gently he tried the handle, it moved, and in one action the door was open and Hunter was in the room.

The noise of Hunter's entry made Kate jump up to her feet, dropping a book on the sofa she had turned to face the intruder. They stood facing each other, tension in the air.

Kate was the first to break the silence. "What are you doing here?" She asked, then more assertively "How dare you break in like that, you scared me, you should have knocked."

Hunter moved further into the room, toward Kate who regaining her composure saw Hunter's injuries.

"What happened to you?" She asked with a tone of compassion in her voice.

"I think you know." Hunter replied. "I just want to know why you handed me over to those thugs."

There was a look of steel in Hunter's eyes, a hard-edged tone to his voice. Kate was scared, she didn't really know this man, and now she felt very vulnerable. Nobody would know he was there, nobody would hear her scream, she backed away. "What do you mean thugs? They were the police."

"Don't play the innocent, you know exactly who they are, what's your connection?"

"I don't know what you mean, they told me they were the police, they wanted me to meet you so they could pick you up."

Hunter laughed, "If they were the police why didn't they just arrest me at the hotel?"

Kate flustered, hearing herself she realised it was stupid, of course they would have just arrested him, but they'd been so convincing, their identity cards looked genuine, what was it they had said, "They, they said that you'd managed to evade them the day before and they wanted to get you when you were distracted, or something like that."

"That's the lamest story I've ever heard, I don't think you're that naive."

"I know, now I'm telling you it does sound strange, keep back!"

Hunter was in front of her now, he pointed to his cheek. "And this is how the Greek police interrogate people? I don't think so."

"I'm sorry," She struggled to get out, her voice breaking. "They told me you were smuggling antiquities and it made me furious, I guess I didn't think beyond that."

Kate's face had gone red, her brow was furrowed and Hunter was sure he could see tears welling up. Either she was a great actress or she was genuine. Hunter took a pace back and his expression mellowed. "It looks like you've been duped, I've been mistaken for someone I'm not and we're both in the shit." Then he smiled. "I'm sorry, I believe you, I just had to be sure. Why don't you get us some drinks, then we can talk this through."

"And something for your face."

Hunter, touched his cheek in a reflex then removed his hand quickly, the blood had dried but the cuts were tender. "Yes I'll wash this blood off in a minute, how about that drink?"

Kate went to the kitchenette and got a couple of beers out of the fridge while Hunter slumped down onto the sofa. Kate handed Hunter an opened bottle and he took a good long drink. "Thanks." He said

Kate pulled up a large cushion and sat on the floor, her legs pulled up, one arm wrapped around her knees pulling them into her chest. She sipped her beer and thought. Hunter was thinking too. He had to trust Kate, she was his only ally but he wasn't sure how she could help him. For the time being at least, her house was a sanctuary.

Hunter looked at Kate and when she looked up at him he asked her "Tell me exactly what they said, how they convinced you that they were the police, what the plan was."

Kate recounted the story. How after she had dropped him off at the hotel she had been approached by a plain cloths police officer, how he had explained that they were a special unit, that they were unsure of the local police, that Hunter was really called Johnson and may have someone in the police working for him. Because of these reasons they wanted her to help them get him in a particular placed distracted and off guard. That he smuggled antiquities to the states that were then sold to private collectors, and how, which she already knew, this was a big problem in Greece and the artefacts were never seen again.

Hunter listened patiently until she had finished then got up and went out side. He lit a cigarette, looked up at the stars and wondered. Then he realised Kate was by his side with another beer. He took it off her, "Thanks." They stood next to each other for a while looking at the stars until Hunter broke the silence, "It figures, they mentioned something about a head, but I didn't know what they were going on about. Could that be a stolen artefact?"

"A head?"

"Yes a head."

"I suppose it could be, if it's an important work in excellent condition it could be worth millions."

"Millions?"

"Yes millions. That would explain why they want to get you, I mean Johnson, so much, that is if they think this Johnson has the head."

"That figures."

"It's not really my area but I do know the Getty museum paid over eighteen million dollars for a statue of Aphrodite, although I think that was Roman, but that was years ago, so if it was something of that calibre who knows, what else did they tell you, did they give you any details?"

"No, they didn't tell me anything, they think I'm Johnson don't forget, and I guess this Johnson knows all about it. It never occurred to me that this was all to do with some old statue. I thought it would be about drugs or something."

"I'll bet they're into that as well, I just want to know about this head. What are we going to do?"

"You're not going to do anything, they know who you are as

well and they're pretty viscous customers. I don't want you getting hurt as well."

"I'm not going to just sit here and do nothing."

"What can we do? We can't go to the police, they already think I'm a lunatic and I doubt if we can get off the island, it's hopeless."

Hunter got up and paced the room while Kate thought.

"Well I'm going to do some research, find out just what it could be they're after, you never know it might just give us an edge."

"While you're researching what will I do, I can't sit around here all day waiting?"

"Do what you came here for."

Hunter looked at her quizzically.

"Be a tourist. Disappear into the crowds."

CHAPTER 4

The next day Hunter found himself in Lindos, a small town, really the size of a village, half way along the east coast of the island, that had originally been founded in the 10th century BC. The whole area was dominated by it's acropolis and the castle that was built by the Knights of St John in the middle ages, below which nestled the whitewashed buildings of the town. Before they had left, Kate had done a rudimentary makeup job on the cuts on his cheeks which were noticeable but camouflaged to any one who did not look at him too closely. Kate had dropped him off in the dusty square outside the town walls where the coach parties disembark, having briefly stopped so that he could buy a new polo shirt, sun-hat and glasses. Once again he hoped that his simple disguise would render him unobtrusive amongst the tourist crowds. He had waited for a coach to disgorge it's load of merry, brightly dressed passengers and infiltrated himself amongst them as they moved from the coach park toward the town. Once they had passed through the arch in the outer wall that provided access to the town's narrow pedestrianised streets, the tourists had spread out in individual groups, some stopping almost immediately to look in shop windows others marching on purposefully, hoping to get to the castle before it was too busy. Hunter was left by himself so he wandered at an idle pace looking down, avoiding eye contact with any passers by, occasionally stooping to look in a shop window but moving on again before he could be harangued into a purchase by an over zealous shopkeeper. Before long the streets widened and Hunter found himself at a crossroads where, without the cover of other tourists he felt suddenly very exposed. He decided to turn left as the road started to go uphill and attempted to keep his pace slow, all the time nervously looking around but trying to disguise the fact. He felt as though a thousand eyes were staring at him, though there were none, so he went into the first cafe he came across, as much to calm himself down as to find cover.

The cafe had no front, the entire wall being a folding glass door which was fully opened, allowing the light to flow in and customers to sit half out on the pavement. It was sparsely furnished with wooden tables and chairs, the walls wood clad to waist height then whitewashed above that. There were framed photographs of scenes of Lindos on the walls, faded and discoloured over time. A tourist couple sat near the front of the cafe, British Hunter suspected, the man had a heavy gold chain around his neck below a shaved head and the woman was exposing a bit too much flesh causing Hunter to shudder inside and wonder "Why?" Toward the back of the cafe were a couple of older locals conversing slowly, looking out to the street, and watching the world go by as they nursed glasses of strong coffee accompanied by larger glasses of water.

Hunter approached the counter that was part ice cream cabinet and ordered a coffee. The assistant a small young Greek girl, her long black hair tied back in a pony tail, dressed in a white halter neck top and black jeans, nodded and turned to an ancient chrome espresso machine while Hunter settled himself at a table halfway down the cafe where he could look out on the road and remain as inconspicuous as possible.

He relaxed, the passers by were just that, there was no one standing on the opposite side of the street observing him, just tourists idling up the road and locals moving more quickly, to get some shopping, or go to work, he didn't know, but anyhow nobody paid the cafe let alone Hunter much attention. The girl brought a small cup of extremely strong coffee and placed it on the table with a till receipt underneath then returned to her station behind the counter. The coffee smelled good so Hunter took a sip screwing his face up as he did so, he'd never tasted coffee so strong and so bitter. He lit a cigarette and sat back half listening to the Euro pop being played on an old transistor radio but more, contemplating what he could do by that evening to avoid whatever it was Marcos had planned for him. The British couple left, flip flopping away down the hill and Hunter took another sip of the outrageous coffee. As he put the coffee cup back down he looked up out of the cafe and saw that an old but respectable looking man with grey hair and a neat grey moustache had stopped outside the cafe and was looking in, directly at Hunter. As soon as the man saw Hunter look up he turned away and walked on out of Hunter's sight.

"Damn!" Hunter thought, "I'm sure he recognised me."

Hunter downed the coffee in one hit dropped some change on the table and headed out of the cafe in the same direction as the grey haired man who he could see not far ahead of him. The road was heading uphill toward the castle and Hunter quite quickly overhauled the man, but instead of stopping Hunter went straight past, ignoring him.

The old man saw Hunter pass but could not keep up the same pace. In fact he was struggling with the hill, so he stopped where another man was selling donkey rides up to the castle. The donkeys were not the usual poor beasts of burden but were well looked after, and gaily festooned with flowers in their manes. The donkey-man helped the old man up onto the saddle and led the donkey forward and up the hill.

Hunter had reached the steps leading up to the castle entrance and took them in twos bounding his way up catching, just by the entrance, a group of tourists who were following a guide. Hunter joined them at the back and as they went into the castle shuffled his way in amongst them.

Meanwhile, the old man still astride the donkey, was led up the steps in his slow motion chase, eventually dismounting by the castle entrance and leaving the donkey with its owner touting for another fare.

Hunter moved with the crowd who paused as the guide started his tour, "Here we can see the medieval ramparts of the castle", but Hunter was not listening, instead trying to see behind without being seen himself. The party moved on, Hunter in their midst, and the old man breathing heavily and unseen by Hunter, followed, trying to pick Hunter out from the crowd.

The group moved up through the castle, the old man trailing behind, until it arrived on the roof and was greeted with spectacular views of the sea and the town spread out below. The group split up into smaller groups and individuals who made their way to the edge of the roof thereby gaining better views. Small digital cameras were produced and people were cajoled into posses to provide some foreground interest in the photographs that would be shown, among the many others, to friends and family or posted on Facebook to say, "I was there, look at what a good time we were having while you were sat at your desk, or in your school or hospital or where ever you were, but certainly not having as good a time as us."

Hunter saw the old man come onto the roof and finding himself once again exposed, and with no where to run, he waited for the old man to approach him, which he did, but instead of stopping he walked right past Hunter seemingly ignoring him but saying to him under his breath, "Follow me!" Hunter was surprised and made to ask a question the words drying on his lips as the old man reached the edge of the roof and took a cursory look at the view before heading back to the steps that led down away from the roof. After a moments pause Hunter followed.

While all this was happening Kate had driven into Rhodes town. She was on a mission, to find out what 'The Head' could be. She parked in the centre of town and made her way to the archaeological museum a building that was familiar to her as she had spent much time there behind the public areas studying texts and objects that only an academic researcher would have access to. The Museum was housed in the medieval building of the Hospital of the Knights. The building dated back to 1440 and was started by Grand Master de Lastic with money bequeathed by his predecessor, Fluvian, and completed in 1489 by Grand Master d'Aubusson. A classical treasure itself, it contained a collection of tomb groups, vases, figurines, jewellery, metal objects, vases and small objects, Classical, Hellenistic and Roman sculpture, mosaic floors of the Hellenistic period from Rhodes town and of the early Christian period from Karpathos and most appropriately for the building itself, funerary slabs from the period of the Knights with relief representations of the dead or of their coats of arms.

Kate could often loose herself in the collection, spending hours in detailed study of an individual object. She loved the building itself, history emanated from it's very fabric and she would soak up the peace and atmosphere letting her imagination run back in time imagining what the world was like when it was built, and further back to the time when the artefacts contained within were first created. Why a girl from Missouri had become so obsessed with Greek classical history was not entirely clear even to Kate herself but she thought it stemmed form the time she was taken to a touring exhibition at the Museum of Art and Archaeology at the University of Missouri in Columbia. The exhibition had so fascinated her that she had from then on spent a lot of time there which had led to her choice of degree, becoming an undergraduate and thence a postgraduate student at that same university. The collection in Missouri was good but here, where the objects had been created and where the history they told of had actually happened, her study felt like more than purely academic research.

Today she lacked the luxury of free time, and headed straight for the academic study area behind closed doors away from the collection and the general public. She made for the office of Professor Konsta, the director of the museum and one of Kate's PhD supervisors. He was a welcoming man, always ready to help, a person who was so immersed in his subject he was almost like one of the permanent exhibits always to be found within the museum. Kate knew nothing about the professor outside academia, whether he had a family or where he lived, as to all intent and purposes he lived in the museum.

Kate knocked on the professor's office door and waited, after a pause she was acknowledged with a distant "come in." She opened the door and was greeted with a familiar scene. The professor's office was a mess. A big desk in the centre of the room was obscured by piles of paper and books. The walls were lined with bookshelves which bowed under the weight of yet more books and papers, in a corner was a small table with a computer and in front of the desk a single chair. The professor was as usual behind his desk studying a paper. He was a small unremarkable looking man, who could have been anything from mid fifties to mid seventies, bald but with a bushy moustache and large thick black framed glasses. He looked up, saw it was Kate, then looked down again at his paper.

Kate sat down on the solitary chair and waited. The professor looked up again and smiled. "What can I do for you?" He asked kindly.

"It's nothing to do with my thesis," Kate said "In fact I'm not sure you can help, but I hope you can."

The professor sat up and paid more attention. "This sounds intriguing, what is it?"

"How much do you know about missing artefacts?" Kate asked.

"It's something that concerns me greatly, over the years many artefacts have gone abroad. In some cases, for minor items that's fine, we can't and wouldn't want to keep everything in the museum, but what's worrying is that more recently some important and unique items have gone missing. If those things are lost to some private collection in the States or China or somewhere they may never be seen again it is a tragedy. Why do you ask? Do you know of something?"

"Possibly, or at least I don't know but want to find out what something may be." Kate replied.

"You'd better tell me what it is and why."

"It's an incredible story but the day before yesterday I met an American tourist on the beach."

"A fellow countryman, there's nothing unusual in that."

Kate blushed, "Maybe not but the strange thing was he came out of the sea fully clothed."

The professor raised his eyebrows, "You'd better tell me the whole story."

Kate then recounted the whole story of the past two days. The professor listened attentively interrupting at times to clarify some detail of time or place. "He then told me that these people think he is someone else, a man called Johnson and, and this is why I've come for your help, they want a head that supposedly Johnson has. I believe this may be a valuable missing artefact and I'm hoping you can help me find out what it is, and if this is all true, if somehow we can get it back."

The professor sat back in his chair and pondered. Kate wanted an answer but had to hold herself back while the professor thought. Eventually he leant forward again. "I've been trying to think what it could be, nothing immediately springs to mind but we have a database of all the valuable missing artefacts, not just from Rhodes but from all of Greece. Let's go through that and see if we can find anything that fits the bill, but I'm afraid it could take a while, it is distressingly long."

The professor got up and went over to his computer, Kate brought her chair over and sat next to him while he opened up the Internet and then the database. "Let's start by value, it must be worth something if these people are so desperate to get their hands on it." So they set to work.

Meanwhile Hunter had followed the old man off the roof and down the steps but instead of returning to the entrance the man turned into the castle, looked around and ducked into an alcove. Hunter followed him into the cool.

"Be at the Kritinia ruins at two and you will discover something that will be to your advantage." The man said and then walked back off to rejoin the crowds on their way down the steps and back into the town.

It had all happened so fast that Hunter's numerous questions dried on his lips. "Oh well," He thought "I've got nothing to loose, but where the hell is Kritinia." Hunter checked his watch, it was eleven thirty. "I've got two and a half hours."

Hunter made his way back to the town and at the first tourist shop went in and bought a map of the island. Outside in the sun he opened it up and looked it over. Kritinia was on the other side of the island, not far, as the island was small, but now he had to find a way there. He walked back down to the coach park in the hope that there may be a bus that went to the other side of the island. All the way down he kept up his guard looking out for anyone in the crowd who looked suspicious, trying to mingle in, but he saw nothing.

The heat was rising and Hunter felt it when he came out of the shaded streets and into the open coach park, it was going to be a hot day. The coach park was half full, some of the coach drivers standing in the shade of a colleagues vehicle chatting and smoking, others dozing in their cabs.

Hunter approached one group, "Does anyone speak English?" He asked. One man nodded. "Do you know if there is a bus for Kritinia?"

The man shook his head, "No you must go back to Rhodes and then take another bus to Megalythos."

"How long will that take?" The coach driver shrugged his shoulders in response, "Thanks, where's the bus stop?" The coach driver pointed to the other side of the coach park where it overlooked a small harbour.

Hunter nodded his thanks and made his way across the square. He found the bus stop and checked the timetable. The next bus was at twelve but took an hour to get to Rhodes, Hunter guessed that it would take the same amount of time to get up the other coast to Kiritinia and that was too tight, even if he jumped from one bus to the other. He needed to find a taxi so he walked back to the coach drivers he had spoken to before.

"Do you know where I can get a taxi?" He asked.

Without replying the coach driver pointed across the square to where a couple of beaten up old cars were parked, their drivers leaning against one of them chatting.

Hunter made his way over, and as he approached their conversation stopped and one of the men opened the back door of his car.

"Kiritinia, please." Hunter asked. The driver's face lit up and he waved Hunter into the back of the car. Inside, the car was as run down as its exterior. The headlining was stained, the floor carpets threadbare, the seats worn with the patina of age. Ahead on the dashboard were snapshots of the driver's family, a cross and a chain of rosary beads hung from the rear view mirror. The driver got in and fired up the engine the noise of which was drowned out by the exhaust which had a hole in and was blowing. The driver engaged first gear, let out the clutch and they trundled off across the car park.

In Professor Konsta's office it was slow work. Kate sat next to the Professor, both of them staring at the computer screen as the professor paged down a list, some with a photograph next to the text others with the photo frame blank. It was a painstaking process as they had to read the descriptions for all the items that didn't have a photograph and some had little detail as they had disappeared long ago. The task was made more difficult as all they had to go on was the one word 'head' and their assumption that it must be valuable.

Hunter meanwhile was not enjoying his journey, the taxi driver was taking the most direct route over the hills. The road was narrow and twisted up and down hill and despite Hunter's assurances to the driver that there was no hurry, he drove as if he was trying to set a time on a rally special stage. More than once they had almost been in the ditch when they had come across another vehicle travelling in the opposite direction and Hunter had almost ended up in the front seat when coming around a blind bend the driver had slammed on the brakes to avoid running in to the back of a slow moving farm trailer. Hunter was regretting not having sat in the front of the car because then he would at least have had a seat belt. Luckily Hunter didn't suffer from motion sickness but even so he hoped the journey would end soon.

The taxi pulled up a steep slope, the driver keeping the car in a low gear, the engine straining at it's maximum revs before cresting the brow after which the road ran straight down to the opposite coast and Hunter sat back and relaxed a little.

Soon they were on the coast road and after a few kilometres the driver turned off and pulled up in the shade of a thicket of pine trees outside the entrance to the ruins of Kiritinia. Hunter felt himself involuntarily exhale, he hadn't realised he'd been holding his breath in, and as he started to breath properly again he felt a wave of relief sweep over him. The taxi driver turned to him and grinned, then held out his hand, Hunter gave him a note, then another and another until the driver was satisfied. Hunter was sure that he'd been ripped off but couldn't argue, instead he got out and waved the taxi driver off as he turned the car around and headed back to the main road in a maelstrom of dust and noise.

Hunter took in his surroundings. There were a few cars parked up under the trees and just off the track a wooden hut by a gate in a chain link fence. This was the entrance to the ruins. Hunter didn't want to go in yet, he was way too early, but he was thirsty so he walked over to the hut to see if he could get a cold drink. The hut had an open shutter and racks of postcards, which depicted the ruins, hung from either side of the opening, discolouring in the bright sunlight. A young woman sat inside the hut listening to pop music that played from a portable radio. Behind her was a shelf covered with guidebooks and to one side a chest freezer. The girl looked up at Hunter with the vacant boredom typical of someone whose days are spent in such circumstances and waited for Hunter to talk.

"Do you have any cold drinks?" Hunter asked.

The girl pointed to a menu on the counter in front of her.

"Lemon Fanta please." Hunter asked, "and an entrance ticket."

The girl opened the chest next to her and passed Hunter an ice cold can, then tore a ticket from a strip, "six Euro." She said with such studied indifference that made Hunter think that whatever unlikely event confronted her, her expression and sloth would stay exactly the same. He wanted to do something to shake her out of her stupor but instead he handed over the money took his drink and ticket and walked back to the shade of the trees. He sat down opened the can and took a drink. It was so cold and fizzy it felt like it first burnt the back of his throat then chilled him down to his stomach as it ran down inside him. He got out a cigarette lit it and took a drag.

A light breeze rustled the pine trees as Hunter alternated between sips of the drink and drags on the cigarette. He checked his watch, he still had plenty of time, and wondered how contact would be made and what he would find out. He wondered how Kate was getting on, he wanted to call her but Marcos had taken his phone the night before so he had no means of contact. He lent back against a tree and lit another cigarette slowly smoking as he drifted into thought. He tried to come up with a plan but every time he did, all that came into his mind was a fantasy image of himself punching Marcos in the face. His mind wandered to the previous days events which led him to feel pangs of guilt for ever having doubted Kate. It was twice now that she had saved him and he hoped that in some way, big or small, he would be able to repay her. His eyes closed and he drifted, not asleep but in a daydream, feeling the cool breeze and enjoying the smell of the pines.

He was disturbed by the arrival of a coach party. First the sound of the vehicle itself then of the passengers as they alighted and made their way inside. He opened his eyes and watched them for a while before checking his watch again, he still had time, but now his siesta had been disturbed he felt restless, beside which the spot where he had placed himself was not the most comfortable, so he decided to go in. He stood up and stretched a little, he hadn't been lying in the best position then walked over to the entrance. He dropped the empty Fanta can in a bin, showed his ticket to the girl, who made a superhuman effort to look up and nod, then walked through the open gates, out of the shade of the trees and into the dry hot air of the ruins. The coach group had spread out in small groups and were dotted around the ruins, the sound of conversations in many languages floating incomprehensibly on the breeze. Before him a series of low ruined stone walls forming the lowest part of long demolished buildings which stretched up and across the hillside in an orderly pattern around a long central thoroughfare. The site was surrounded on three sides by pine trees and looking downhill Hunter could see the sea. The whole site was around four hundred yards across and eight hundred long. He paused to take it all in, it was a beautiful place and he tried to imagine how it might of been all those centuries ago when it was still inhabited.

"What now?" Hunter thought. "Where do I go?" There was no obvious meeting place, no one with a banner pointing at them saying "HERE!" so he decided to walk around like the tourists and wait to find out. Whoever was going to contact him must have an idea of what he looked like so he would have to leave it to them. He walked straight into the heart of the ancient city. Unlike the other visitors he carried no guidebook, and paid little attention to the ruins themselves, instead he scanned the city looking for a signal, a sign of contact, wondering where and how that contact would be made.

It was hot. Hunter wished he had brought some water. He stopped took off his hat and sunglasses, wiped away the perspiration that ran down into his eyes from his forehead, and looked around again. Nothing. Presently Hunter found himself on the main thoroughfare that ran the entire length of the city, up the hill, to what he assumed must have been a temple or palace. He checked his watch, time was up, so he looked around again staring directly at anyone who was within sight trying to see if there was some sort of reaction or obvious signal to tell him that that person was his contact. But nothing, they were all in groups engaged in their own conversations and didn't notice the solitary figure looking at them. Having drawn a blank he started to walk up the thoroughfare toward the top of the hill. Then when he saw another man some way up ahead of him, he paused. The man was too far away for Hunter to see exactly what he looked like but he was of a similar height and build to Hunter with dark hair and wearing sunglasses, Wayfarers like Hunter's. The man seemed to recognise Hunter then darted off on a side path through the ruins. Hunter knew this must be the person he was there to see so he started to walk briskly up the road to where the man had been, then turned off in the same direction. The path was narrow and at this point filled with shade from the walls of the ruins which were too high for Hunter to see over. The path made a turn to the right and as Hunter turned he saw the other man waiting for him at the next bend. Seeing Hunter the man immediately started off again. Hunter followed increasing his pace and starting to get annoyed with what he saw as a ridiculous subterfuge but despite that, Hunter followed the path through the ruins as it started to work its way uphill. He didn't see the man again and wondered if maybe he had made a mistake, maybe this wasn't the person who wanted to see him. Nevertheless he continued to wind his way thorough the deserted pathways. He turned a corner and came across a young couple kissing, the girl pressed against the low wall, her partner leaning against her. Hunter tried to look the other way as he passed but he needn't have worried, they were oblivious to anything except each other. Soon the path led him out of the ruins. He was in a slightly elevated position out on the opposite side of the ruins to the entrance where small groups from the coach party were already leaving. He looked around for the other man, and spotted him making his way up to the high point at the top of the city.

Rather than returning to the maze of ruins Hunter set off through a cool sweet smelling grove of pine trees and skirted the ruins as he headed up hill to a point where he hoped he would converge with the other man or, if not, be able to look down and spot him.

Soon the pine trees thinned and Hunter was again out in the open, he kept going crouching slightly to try to make himself as inconspicuous as possible and within a few minutes he arrived at the head of the city. He stood in the welcomely refreshing breeze and looked down the hill to the sea, the whole ruined town spread out in front of him. He could see a few tourists at the far end of the central avenue and the heads of others moving around within the walls but he could not see the man he had been attempting to follow. He looked around behind him to a landscape of rolling green hills dotted with olive and pine groves, where in the distance a farmer led a donkey laden with wood, it was a timeless scene and one that he might have seen in an old master painting, but still he could not see the man.

Hunter turned back to the city and there right in front of him he saw himself.

To describe Hunter's reaction as one of astonishment would be something of an understatement. He was flabbergasted. He realised his mouth was hanging open so closed it, blinked to make sure he wasn't seeing things and stood staring dumfounded.

The other man smiled. "I can see now why Marcos has been chasing you all over the island, not quite as good looking as me but it's close. We could have been separated at birth."

Hunter noticed that the man's accent was not Mid West like his but more East Coast. He was also a little shorter, a little bulkier, and when he smiled his eyes stayed cold and hard. He couldn't deny the similarity though, they could have been near identical twins, now he understood why he had been mistaken for him.

"You're Johnson!?" Hunter both stated and asked.

Johnson nodded. "If that's what you want to call me that's who I am."

"That's what, what did you call him, Marcos, called you."

Johnson shrugged, "That's what he calls me, but it's not important."

If he didn't already hate this man for the trouble he had caused and the situation he had put him in, Hunter soon would have. He immediately disliked Johnson's superior, arrogant manner, his overconfidence and above all the cold look in his eyes that told of a deeper evil.

"So why all the cloak and dagger stuff, what do you want with me."

"I like to be in control of the situation, you're an innocent caught up in an intrigue that really doesn't concern you. On the other hand it concerns me greatly and you unwittingly have and will contribute to the successful conclusion of the enterprise. It's lucky for me that you turned up when you did you've made my life easier."

"I really don't care. I don't care about you or what you're up to, I don't care about intrigues or Marcos or any of it. Damn the lot of you." Hunter burst out angrily.

"Shut up and listen! You'd better get used to the fact that you're going nowhere until this is all settled so you'd better calm down and start co-operating, that is if you want to leave here alive oh and save your girlfriend."

"You leave her out of this."

"She's already in it and you're responsible. Now I need you to do me a favour."

"No chance." Hunter replied, "I wouldn't help you if...if..." A suitable simile escaped Hunter.

"I think you have little choice, if you don't help me I'll make sure the police know you are me and what you, I, have done. Then you'll be spending some time in a Greek gaol, that is of course if I don't let Marcos know where you are, and you already know how he operates. So shut up and listen!" Johnson ordered.

Hunter knew he didn't have any options, for the moment he was defeated, he rationalised that it was better to go along with things for now and wait for an opportunity to present itself. He raised a hand in contrition and nodded. "Go on then I may as well hear what you've got planned."

"Right," Johnson paused, "I'm glad you are starting to see sense. I expect you want to know what this is all about. Let's get in the shade and I'll tell you."

Johnson led Hunter over to the pine trees and into the shade, then turned and faced Hunter who now had his back to the ancient city and the sea. Johnson kept half an eye on Hunter and half looking out over the ruins as he spoke. "I used to work with Marcos, I have a knowledge of antiquities and contacts in the States, collectors, private, discreet and wealthy clients who always have an eye and the cash for something rare, something special or beautiful. Well I soon realised that I would become a lot wealthier a lot more quickly if I cut out the middleman, well I'm the middleman so lets say the lower level of the organisation..."

"Marcos?"

"Exactly, so when he got hold of a certain item of particular value, the opportunity was to good to miss. I stole it from the thief and returned to the States to arrange the sale. My only problem was getting back to collect the merchandise, and getting it off the island discreetly, without being caught. Now here I am so the first part went well, but the second is trickier. You've complicated things. They didn't know I was here, but now they think you are me, they are alerted and looking out, for me. So you've caused me a bit of a problem but by so doing you may have solved a bigger one. If they've got you they won't be looking for me."

"And that's your plan? Give me to Marcos so you can escape? It doesn't sound to good for me." Hunter was almost laughing at the absurdity of the situation.

Johnson gave him his hollow smile. "I guess not, but Marcos will find you anyway, and if you help me, once I'm away I'll make sure he knows that you're you and not me, it's the best chance you've got."

"You know I think I'll just go to the police and tell them the whole story." Hunter bluffed.

"They'll just give you the cold shoulder like before."

Hunter looked surprised.

Johnson laughed. "I like to know what's going on and I have my network of informers, so I knew about you when you arrived and I know that the police didn't want to help you."

Hunter shook his head, his face showed defeat, then he made a sudden lunge for Johnson who sidestepped him tripping him to the ground. Hunter rolled onto his back to be faced by Johnson standing over him an automatic pistol in his hand pointing directly at Hunter's head.

Johnson's manner was less friendly now. "You're a bloody amateur, not even an amateur, a no one, now what's it going to be?"

Now Hunter did feel defeated, he raised his hands slowly and nodded. "Ok, tell me what you want me to do."

Johnson slipped the gun back into his jacket, then held out his hand and helped Hunter to his feet. "Very sensible. Now listen."

CHAPTER 5

In the archaeological museum the morning dragged, Professor Konsta worked his way through the database while Kate sat expectantly watching him, from time to time leaning over to see what he was looking at when he paused to study an entry in more detail, but all their searches were fruitless. Eventually he looked up from the computer his face an expression of apology.

"I'm sorry there's nothing here that it could obviously be, if it is an artefact they must have something that we don't know about and if that's the case, it's even more important that it is recovered, but I'm not sure what we can do."

"What about the police don't you think that they'll be interested?"

The professor thought for a moment. "The special unit in Athens certainly will be, as for the local police, from what you've told me it may be counter productive to talk to them. I'll contact the Athens unit but with so little to go on I'm not sure what they can do. You'll admit the story is a little fantastic. A strange American being chased across the island by a gang in pursuit of a missing antiquity that we don't even know exists? What would you think?"

Kate thought about the professor's remarks for a moment, "You're right of course, put like that I'm not sure I'd believe it, but, if you'd met this man you would. I do."

The professor smiled, "He's had an effect on you hasn't he?"

Kate blushed slightly, "Yes, he has."

"Can you stay for a while until I can contact the Athens office and find out if they know anything or can help?"

"No, I need to get going, I've arranged to meet John and let him know what I've found out."

"Well please don't get too involved, you don't know this man and I would hate you to put yourself in any danger, be careful."

"Thank you for your concern, I'll try not to."

Kate made her goodbyes and left the professor to contact the specialist unit and go back to his studies. His words resonated as she walked out through the museum. She was worried. Was she being naive? Could she really trust this man or was she getting herself involved in something she really shouldn't? She was soon to find out.

Kate had agreed to meet Hunter at the Butterfly Valley, a tourist attraction in the middle of the island. It was a place where they were unlikely to be found or arouse any suspicion and as it was so busy with tourists unlikely that anything could happen there. It was a half-hour drive from Rhodes town and Kate made the journey without taking in anything of the surroundings, her thoughts preoccupied by the situation in which she found herself.

When she arrived the car park was almost full. She drove around for a while until she managed to find a spot right in the middle away from the shade of the trees. The car park was on the side of a hill surrounded by woods and on the down hill side, above and through the trees was a far reaching view of farmlands stretching to the rocky mountains of the south of the island.

Kate made her way to the entrance where there was a short queue. Once she reached the front she paid the fee then made her way with the other visitors into the trees on a wooden path that wound it's way uphill along the course of a stream. The trees were full of butterflies that when they were disturbed, momentarily lifted off in great swarms before landing again, their yellow brown and green colours camouflaging them against the leaves and wood of the trees. She took her time walking at the pace of the other tourists, stopping at appropriate places to watch the butterflies, to anyone watching she was just one of the tourist crowd. After a while the path turned back down hill, Kate followed it and after what must have been half an hour in total found herself back at the start. She looked around attempting to be subtle then made her way to a cafe which was located next to the entrance. The cafe which was full of tourists enjoying a late lunch or a cool drink, had a veranda that opened out onto the southern vista. She found a table sat down and checked her watch. Hunter should have been there by then and Kate wondered what might have happened to delay him.

A waiter approached breaking Kate's train of thought, she ordered a coffee and a sandwich and sat back to wait.

Meanwhile at the ruins of Kiritinia, Hunter was still listening to Johnson. "So you've got it?" Johnson said.

"Yes I've got it." Hunter replied, at which point he felt a sharp blow on the head then nothing more as he fell to the ground unconscious.

Kate waited at the cafe. People came and went, the waiter came and went, bringing Kate a series of drinks and snacks. It wasn't that she wanted them but she had to buy something so that she could keep her place at the cafe. The air started to cool and the sun passed behind the trees throwing the cafe into shade. Still there was no sign of Hunter and his appearance wasn't hastened by Kate's regular reference to her watch.

Still Kate waited until she was the only one left on the veranda. The sun was starting to set when the waiter approached. "We are closed now." He said and with a nod and a smile Kate gave him the money for the bill, got up and left.

The car park was now almost empty. There was no artificial light and it was rapidly getting dark. Kate could see her car isolated in the middle of the parking area, almost all the other vehicles having left, and started towards it. All of a sudden she stopped, and sensing something looked around. She couldn't see anything in the shadows but she was spooked. She started to run toward her car straight in to a large man who had stepped out of the shadows in front of her. The man grabbed her by the arms and despite her struggles he was too strong and she could not free herself. A large dark saloon car pulled up next to them, the back door opened and Kate was bundled in. It had taken seconds and despite her caution Kate was now a hostage.

She found herself next to Marcos and was pushed into the middle by one of the men, Xenephon, who had chased Hunter on his arrival and who she recognised as one of the bogus policemen who had got her to lure Hunter to the Son et Lumière, he got in after her she was trapped.

The large man got in the passenger seat and the car drove off into the rapidly approaching night.

Kate's heart raced, the words of professor Konsta rang in her ears. She didn't know what these people would do and she was scared.

Once they were away from the butterfly valley Marcos turned to her, "You're very foolish." He started, "Johnson's used you beautifully, I have to admire him really, but you should know, he's a ruthless character he's been using you and due to your help he's managed to evade us. He should be back in touch soon, but you may be of use for information or as a hostage but knowing Johnson, he won't help you unless it helps him. We're not very happy about that and if you've got any sense you'll help us find him again."

"I don't know any Johnson." Kate said defiantly.

"Oh come on," Marcos was mocking, "I don't know what he told you and really I don't care, he's a liar and a thief, and you shouldn't have got involved with him. However whatever you do know may help us and Maria will have great fun finding out."

Kate hadn't noticed the woman driving until at that moment Maria turned around and licking her lips gave Kate an evil grin.

Kate looked straight ahead trying not to show any fear. She

CHAPTER 5

didn't know what was going to happen but she knew it wouldn't
be good. Again professor Konsta's words echoed through her
mind, "Don't put yourself in any danger."

Nothing more was said for the rest of the journey. Kate felt the
tension and fear grow with every passing mile until she felt fit to
burst, her hands clenched tight. She tried to calm herself down,
relaxing her hands, breathing more deeply concentrating on
bringing down her heart rate, but in the pit of her stomach she
felt it.

When the car stopped Marcos and Maria got out first before
Kate was pulled out by the large man. He led her into the
building and into the office where Hunter had been taken
the night before. Kate looked around, the desk was large with
carved wooden legs, and nothing on it. Behind the desk was
a leather chair and in front a plain wooden chair. Otherwise
the room was completely unfurnished except for a set of heavy
curtains that covered the only window which was set in the
wall behind the desk. The floor was tiled and the walls painted
white. Kate was directed to sit down, which she did and the
man retreated to stand by the door.

Kate's mind raced, her thoughts going back to Hunter and the
condition he had been in when he appeared the previous night.
She didn't have to wait long, the door opened and Marcos and
Maria came into the room. Marcos sat down behind the desk
and Maria stood behind Kate.

"Tell me now and it will be better for you" Marcos said, "Where
is Johnson?"

"I don't know who Johnson is," Kate's reply was cut short as

Maria grabbed her hair and pulled it back with a jolt. Kate's face reddened but she was determined not to show how much it hurt her.

"Maria hates liars, you'd better start answering correctly."

"I'm not lying." Kate let out as Maria pulled her head back further. Kate thought she would break her neck and gasped in pain. Maria eased off but didn't let go of Kate's hair.

"Make it easy on yourself, tell me where Johnson is, and where the head is." Marcos demanded.

Kate didn't reply, her face was flushed, her eyes watering, but she stared defiantly and directly back at Marcos.

Marcos shook his head with mock exasperation and tuted under his breath. "It's a shame, you've got such a pretty face. I'd hoped you'd be more sensible, now I'm going to have to let Maria enjoy herself with you. I've wasted enough of my time."

With this Marcos got up and left the room, stopping on his way to address the guard quietly but deliberately loud enough so that Kate could hear. "Stay here and make sure she doesn't get too carried away."

Maria let go of Kate's hair and sat on the edge of the desk her eyes alight with dark intent.

Kate was scared and at that point if she'd known anything she would have blurted it out, but there was nothing she could say that would help her.

Hunter had come around in pitch darkness. He found himself lying on a bare floor, cold from the tiles. As he sat up he felt the pain in his head, touched the point where he had been hit and flinched. He felt his way across the floor to a wall where he could sit up with support. He felt around in his pockets and found his cigarettes and lighter. "That wasn't so bright." He thought to himself. He pulled out a cigarette and lit it. He took a deep drag, then fired the lighter again and took in his surroundings. Nothing, an empty room, tiled floor white walls, a heavy wood door and one window the shutters closed and he assumed locked. He let the lighter go out and smoked in darkness. At that moment he couldn't think, his splitting headache was all he could concentrate on. The cigarette finished, Hunter just sat there, immobile, he felt any fight had been knocked out of him. He'd got himself into a mess and now he had run out of ideas. He checked his watch, it was gone six and he suddenly remembered Kate and their rendezvous. Hopefully she had realised something had happened and gone home, but some feeling told him that something had happened to her. Now he was worried more for Kate than for himself. After a while he forced the negative thoughts out of his mind, sitting there worrying wouldn't get him anywhere, he had to come up with a plan. With a considerable effort he got to his feet and walked to the other side of the room where he checked the shutters, sure enough they wouldn't budge. Next he tried the door, gently trying to turn the handle but it was, as he had known it would be, locked. Defeated, he sat down again, on the floor behind the door, and held his aching head in his hands.

After some time he heard footsteps. All of a sudden his senses were alive, his body tense with expectation, his headache momentarily forgotten, he got up into a crouched position and waited, ready. The footsteps came nearer then stopped outside the door. A key was inserted in to the lock and turned, then light shone into the room as the door opened and as a figure started to enter Hunter leapt up slamming the door with all the force he could muster, crushing the figure between it and the door frame. Hunter pulled the door back open, bent over what was a man, pulled him up by the jacket with his left hand and hit him with a huge right hook before dropping him back on the floor unconscious. Taking a moment to get his eyes accustomed to the light Hunter looked out through the door into a corridor. There was no one else in sight so with a snap decision he turned left and made his way hurriedly down the corridor. He quickly found an external door which by good fortune was unlocked and within moments he was outside and running straight toward a nearby grove of pine trees which were just a dark silhouette against the night sky.

Once he was in the trees he paused to regain his breath and to take his bearings. Looking back from where he had come he could see lights shining through the windows of several rooms of the building and realised he didn't have time to wait. Gathering himself he made his way briskly further into the trees.

It wasn't long before Johnson had realised the footsteps he had just heard in the corridor were not of his assistant coming back to report. He came out into the corridor and saw a pair of legs protruding from the doorway to the room where Hunter was supposedly being kept. He knew immediately that Hunter had escaped but still went over to check. The man was out cold in the doorway, the room was empty. Johnson uttered a curse and for good measure gave the recumbent figure a vicious kick in the ribs. He turned on his heels and shouted out for help.

In the woods, Hunter heard the shout and moved more quickly. He was still dazed from the blow he had received earlier in the day and was running only on adrenaline but even that was running out. He paused and leant against a tree in an attempt to regain his breath, at that moment the situation suddenly seemed almost funny, he suppressed a laugh, almost as much of despair as humour as he looked at his predicament from the outside. Then he heard his pursuers coming out of the building, he pulled himself together and started running again.

Johnson had come out of the building with his accomplice and paused at the edge of the trees, listening, all he could hear were the sounds of the night. The trees creaked as they swayed in the breeze, the cicadas hummed and in the distance an owl hooted. He directed his man to go around in one direction and he himself went in the other skirting around the wood. After a few hundred metres he paused again, then he heard another noise. It was the sound of feet falling on the dry leaves and earth of the forest floor. He spent a moment identifying where the sound was coming from then waited. The footsteps were coming toward him and the next moment Hunter burst out from the trees and stopped dead in front of him.

"Not you again." Hunter said with a tone of ironic humour.

"Come on." Johnson replied, "you might as well give it up."

Hunter started to lift his hands in surrender then in an instant smashed Johnson on the head with a tree branch that he had picked up in the wood and Johnson, in the dark, hadn't seen. Johnson collapsed in a heap.

"That's for yesterday, and ruining my holiday and...whatever."

Hunter said. He knelt down next to Johnson and rummaged through his pockets, "Damn no car keys." Then he got up and headed toward the building. After a few paces he stopped and turned back to Johnson. He crouched down and quickly stripped Johnson of his shirt, shoes and trousers, then stripped off himself. He put on Johnson's clothes and put his clothes on Johnson. Then headed back toward the building. In the corridor the man he had slammed in the door was now sitting up, his jaw swelling blue and purple. "Good punch." Hunter thought to himself. He stood over the man.

"Where are the car keys?" He demanded.

The man was dazed and now confused. This was Johnson standing over him but his voice had changed. He made to stand up and Hunter kicked him full force in the jaw. The man collapsed again.

Hunter turned back down the corridor and checked in each room until he found an office. He rummaged through the drawers and quickly found a set of keys. He grabbed them and then paused, next to the keys was a revolver, for a moment he was uncertain then he picked it up and went back outside. He walked around to the front of the building where a car was parked, it was unlocked so he jumped in. The keys fitted the ignition so without pausing he started it up and drove off.

Johnson came around felt his head, and found a damp patch of blood already congealing in his hair. "Bastard!" he exclaimed then got up, his legs unstable beneath him and started toward the building at which moment his accomplice coming out of the woods saw him and mistaking him for Hunter grabbed him from behind. "Boss, boss, I've got him!" He shouted.

Johnson was apoplectic. "You idiot! Let go of me now!" He stopped as he heard the car drive off. "You fool he's taken the car, let go of me!"

The man was confused but let go, Johnson turned and slapped him hard around the face, then marched toward the building. "Come with me! Idiot."

Hunter had driven out of the building's driveway and made a quick decision which way to turn. He chose left. Either way he would at sometime end up at the sea and hope to recognise where he was and therefore take the right direction on the coast road, in the meantime he wanted to put as much distance between himself and Johnson as quickly as possible.

Sure enough after about fifteen minutes he arrived at the sea. "Was this the east or west coast?" He wasn't sure so again he made a guess and turned right. There was an intermittent flow of cars on the coast road so Hunter settled down to the rhythm of the traffic, keeping up with it's pace, not dawdling or going so fast as to attract attention. It wasn't long before he thought he recognised the landscape, difficult though it was in the dark and soon came upon a road junction he definitely recognised. He turned off the coast road and was soon driving up the track to Kate's house. He pulled up and got out. There was something about the scene that bothered him, call it intuition or sixth sense but something felt wrong. He crouched and looked around then he realised what was bothering him. Kate's car was not there and there was no tell tale chink of light through the shutters. He looked down and saw the revolver tucked into his trousers paused momentarily then pulled it out and checked that there was a round in the chamber. He also checked where the safety catch was. It was on and he breathed a sigh of relief and kicked himself for not checking before, after what had been going on accidentally shooting himself would have been the final icing on the cake.

Gun in hand he crept up to the house. There were no lights showing so he made his way around to the back and checked the French windows, which were locked. He went back 'round to the front and tried the front door, it too was locked. Then he knocked, at first gently then louder. There was no movement inside and Hunter was forced to conclude as he had anyway suspected, that there was no one inside. "What now?"

In Marcos's office Kate was slumped back in the chair, her hair was a mess, her face red and her eyes were wet. She had been roughed up not badly beaten but even so it wasn't a happy experience. At least Maria hadn't damaged her like she had Hunter.

Maria sat behind the desk grinning at Kate. "Are you going to cry little girl?" She asked mockingly.

Kate didn't bother to look up, she didn't want Maria to see her tears. Maria laughed at her, "You have no idea what I could do to you do you? When I've finished with you, you'll be begging for mercy, I'm, what do you call it, a sadist?"

Kate tried to be strong but inside she was shaking. "How," she thought, "did I get myself into this?"

The door opened and Marcos came back into the room. Maria got out of his seat and stood to one side. Marcos addressed Kate. "So what do you want to tell me now?"

Kate didn't look up, instead summoning her inner defiance she muttered under her breath, "Go to hell."

Marcos shook his head, then turned to Maria. "You've been too gentle, we don't have time to waste." With which he left the room again. Maria her mouth open in a twisted smile approached Kate who instinctively drew herself back into the chair and tensed.

Hunter meanwhile sat by the swimming pool outside Kate's house smoking and pondering. He had moved the car away from the house into some trees where it was hidden from sight, he wasn't sure whether Johnson or Marcos now knew where Kate's house was and he wanted to get away without them realising he had been there if they did turn up. His head was still aching from the blow he'd received earlier and what he really wanted was a good drink and a comfortable bed. Instead he smoked and wondered what had become of Kate. He'd missed their meeting and all he could think was that she would have come back to her house, unless.....

Kate bit hard on the gag. Her arms were tied behind her, tight to the back of the chair, her bare feet tied to the table, the soles exposed. Maria hit them again with the thin switch of branch. The soles of Kate's feet seared with the pain that instantaneously transmitted itself throughout her body causing it to twitch, her eyes involuntarily watering and her brain cried for it to stop. Thwack! Maria caned Kate's feet, and again and again until Kate thought she would pass out.

Hunter checked his watch, he'd been waiting over an hour. He was pretty sure now that Kate wasn't going to turn up and she wasn't going to turn up because either, he hoped she was staying somewhere else, hidden out of the way and out of danger, or else, and this is what he believed to be the truth, Marcos had kidnapped her. How he could find Marcos place he did not know. He'd tried to follow the way when he'd been blindfolded the night before but it had been impossible. He sat in indecision and realised just how hungry and thirsty he was but unless he broke in, which he didn't want to do, he just had to bear it. It didn't make sense to sit where he was though so he got up checked the safety on the revolver and stuck it back in his trousers then made his way to where he had left the car. He had positioned it so that it was facing down the track, ready for a quick getaway and from the drivers seat he had a clear view of the entrance to the house. He got in put the keys in the ignition, the revolver on his lap and settled down to wait. Either Kate would come back, or someone else would come, either way there was nothing else he could do.

Kate was swimming in and out of consciousness, when the door opened. "That's enough." She heard Marcos say, "Untie her feet."

Kate felt her feet released, she put them down on the floor and felt some relief from the cool of the tiles. She didn't look up, she had had it. Instead she sat slumped in the chair enjoying, as much as it was possible the cool tiles soothing her feet.

"Alright," She heard Marcos say, "Now maybe you'll tell me, where is Johnson and where is the head?"

Kate's spirit was broken, all she wanted was to be away from these people, to go back to her house and sleep, to forget any of this had happened. She looked up at Marcos through her dishevelled hair. She took a deep breath and started to speak.

Her voice was almost a whisper. "We were going to meet at the butterfly valley but he never turned up. The man you've been chasing isn't Johnson..."

"Not that again." Marcos interrupted.

"You've got to believe me!" Kate shouted. "He isn't Johnson."

Marcos was so surprised at the force of Kate's statement that he leant back in his chair, and pondered for a while, "Alright go on."

"The man you think is Johnson, isn't, he just looks like him, you've been chasing the wrong person, he's just a tourist I met on the beach called Hunter and I don't know anything about any head."

"Where is this Hunter then?" Marcos demanded.

"I don't know." Kate replied "He never turned up at the butterfly valley, instead you did." She paused for thought. "How did you know I'd be there?"

"Don't you remember? When you thought we were the police you told us everything, it wasn't hard to follow you."

There was nothing else she could tell him and her silence annoyed Marcos.

"You're not helping very much," Said Marcos, "Shall I tell you what I think?" The question was rhetorical. "I think that you are in league with Johnson, that you are helping him find the buyers, after all you are an archaeologist and an American."

Kate looked up. "How do you know that?"

"Don't interrupt." Marcos ordered. "So who better to help someone who smuggles antiquities, especially with your cover. Now be sensible admit it and tell me where he is."

Kate struggled for thought, "But if I was his accomplice why would I have given him to you at the Son et Lumière? I wouldn't have done that would I?"

Marcos thought for a moment. "Maybe you're smarter than you look and were thinking of double crossing him like he double crossed me? I don't know and I don't care I just want the head." he paused then his tone changed "No you're not that smart, naieve, stupid. Alright, supposing for a moment you are telling the truth, you wouldn't care about Johnson would you?"

Seeing an opening Kate perked up, "No I hate him, I hate what he does and...and.."

"So you'll help me to find him?"

Kate realised she was trapped but had been given a lifeline, "Yes, yes I will."

"Good. Maria take her away and clean her up, I need to think."

Maria untied Kate from the chair. Kate slipped on her sandals and tried to stand up. She felt the pain in the soles of her feet and sat down again. Maria put her hands under Kate's armpits and lifted her to her feet. Kate was unsteady, her feet were very painful. To Kate's surprise Maria lent her a shoulder and put her arm around Kate's waist and helped her out of the room. She took her to a bathroom and locked the door behind her. Kate sat down on the toilet put her head in her hands and cried. The fear and the beating had broken her, she was overwhelmed. She sobbed uncontrollably her whole body shaking spasmodically. Then as if the water flooding through a burst dam had levelled out behind the breach her tears stopped. She stood up with difficulty and looked at herself in the mirror, the face that looked back was not familiar, her hair was all over the place sticking up in places and falling down her face in others. Her face was puffy, her eyes red with dark rings around them, she looked a mess, but the thing that struck Kate most about her reflection was that she looked harder. She couldn't define exactly how but some of the bright carefree look that she usually saw had gone. She tried to smile at herself but it was a forced, weak and untrue smile. She ran the tap and splashed some cold water in her face then picked up a convenient hairbrush and pulled it through her hair. She worked out the knots and scraped it back. When she had finished she smiled at herself again and saw a more familiar face look back at her. There was no more to do except go to the toilet. When she had finished she knocked on the door which was opened by Maria who had been waiting outside and who led her back to the office.

When they entered, Marcos was in place behind his desk and with a wave of the hand he signalled to Kate to sit down which she did. Marcos looked her over.

"So you were to meet at the Butterfly Valley. We had assumed that, which is why we followed you. But he didn't show up. There is no second man, think about it. I know Johnson well and I am sure the man who arrived here two days ago is Johnson. Could there be someone who looks identical, who just happens to turn up here on vacation, when we are expecting him? It is inconceivable. You have been taken for a fool and used by Johnson. I think that he has used you as a diversion while he tried to escape, but I think he is still here, lying low. I also think that wherever he went, it was to take delivery of the head from whoever has had it hidden and now he's got it he doesn't need you any more. I'm not sure but for the moment I'll accept that you are an unwitting accomplice, but save yourself further pain and embarrassment and if he is still on the island help us find him."

Marcos's reasoning made absolute sense and Kate questioned whether she had indeed been taken for a fool, but something told her that Hunter was genuine, however she felt she had little choice but to help Marcos, she didn't want to go through her experience with Maria a second time.

"Well?" Marcos was waiting.

"I don't know?" Kate replied. She wasn't playing for time, she really didn't know what to say.

"It might help you to know that yesterday he was here and we let him go so that he could recover the head and bring it to us. He agreed, but it seems that he didn't fulfil his side of the agreement and has given us you instead. Don't you think if he was at all bothered about you he would have turned up this afternoon?"

Kate nodded her agreement.

"Now let's start with where you live. If he wanted a safe place to hide that's where he would go."

Kate was reluctant to tell Marcos where her home was but she realised she didn't have a choice. She described how to get there and as she did so wished she could somehow warn Hunter.

"Give me your keys!" Marcos demanded.

"They're in my bag." Kate replied.

Marcos opened a drawer and pulled out Kate's bag, he rummaged around inside until he found a bunch of keys. He held them up to Kate who nodded. Then Marcos signalled to the man who all the time had been standing by the door. "Get Xenophon and go over there. Be careful, if Johnson is there he probably won't be alone and he will be armed. If he is there bring him back here." The man nodded and left the room.

"So now we wait." Marcos said.

Hunter was half asleep when he heard the car. It was in the distance on the main road but unlike the few other cars that had passed since he had been sitting there, this one had stopped. He opened his eyes and let them adjust to the dark. Then he waited. Sure enough after a couple of minutes a tall bulky figure appeared on the track. He proceeded slowly and Hunter was convinced he could make out the silhouette of a gun in the mans hand. Hunter held the revolver more tightly and slid a little lower in his seat. One thing was for sure, it wasn't Kate. Cautiously the man approached the house but he didn't go to the front door. Instead as Hunter himself had done the man went around the side of the house, reappearing after a couple of minutes. Then to Hunter's surprise the man took some keys from his pocket, opened the front door and went in. Hunter was so absorbed in watching the man at the house he wasn't looking in the rear view mirror and didn't see a second man approach the car from behind. Suddenly Hunter's door was pulled open and a gun was pointing in his face.

"Don't make a move." The man said quietly then gently lifted the revolver from Hunter's hand.

They stayed in that position for a few minutes until the first man came back out of the house.

"Alexandros, over here." Xenophon said under his breath. Alexandros looked around saw his companion and came over to the car.

"Was there any one else inside?"

"No, nothing."

Then to Hunter Xenophon ordered. "Get out!"

Hunter obeyed, getting out very carefully and putting his hands on his head to make it clear he wasn't going to cause any trouble.

"Check the car over!" Xenophon ordered Alexandros.

Alexandros turned on the interior lights and made a thorough search. When he had finished he opened the bonnet and with a torch looked around the engine bay. He then crouched down and checked under the car before finally opening the boot and checking it over, lifting the carpet up and the spare wheel out to make sure there was nothing there. When he had finished he shrugged at Xenophon. "Nothing." He said.

"Ok lets take him back." Then to Hunter "Come on, down the track, we'll be right behind you."

Hunter walked down the track his hands still over his head, with the two men following, guns pointing at Hunter's back. At the bottom of the track a car was parked blocking the entrance. "They're no mugs." Hunter thought to himself before Xenophon opened the back door. "Get in," he ordered. Hunter complied and was followed into the back seat by Xenophon who kept his handgun pointing at Hunter. Alexandros got in the front and with no further ado he started the car and headed off back to the coast road.

More than an hour had passed when Kate heard footsteps in the corridor outside the office. She looked around to the door. The footsteps stopped, the door opened and Hunter was pushed in.

"John." Kate exclaimed.

"Johnson." Said Marcos.

Hunter was followed in by Xenophon and Alexandros who shut the door behind them.

"No, Hunter." Hunter said defiantly.

"Still the pretence? Come on let's stop playing games." Marcos demanded. Hunter ignored him and turned to Kate.

"Are you all right?" he asked.

"I'll survive." She replied.

"Very touching." Marcos interjected. "I'm getting fed up with all this. Where have you got the head?"

Hunter was still looking at Kate and made an apologetic face, before turning to Marcos. Kate didn't know what it meant until he spoke.

"If I tell you will you let her go?" He asked.

"No John, it's not true!" Kate burst out.

"Shut up!" Hunter let out. "I'm not talking to you."

Kate was shocked. Maybe Marcos had been right all along, she had been a fool but she couldn't believe it. The man, she now realised that she had fallen for, turned out to be a criminal of the worst sort. John, Johnson, it seemed obvious. Why had she been so stupid? As she thought all this, the conversation continued.

Marcos smiled. "At last you're starting to see good sense. It's a shame you didn't before, we had a good operation, if you hadn't got greedy..." He trailed off as if he was remembering a past failed love then brought himself back. "It's not like you to worry about someone else, in the past you've been ruthless, why are you bothered about the girl?"

"Think about it," Hunter was thinking on his feet, "she's an American, she's well known, if anything happens to her, there'll be a hell of a fuss."

"You're right of course, but she knows who we are, you should never of involved her in the first place." He paused for thought.

"We'll decide what to do with her when you've returned the head. In the meantime Maria will look after her. Now are you back on board with us, are you going to tell us where the head is or not?"

Hunter couldn't press the point, he had an inkling of a plan and for it to work he needed Marcos to continue to believe that he was Johnson.

"I can tell you, but it's a hard place to find, besides my guys are there and I've told them to get out if anyone comes except me and you."

Marcos thought about this for a moment. "So you want me to go alone with you? I don't think so, I'm not that stupid. Call them and tell them the plan has changed and you want them to bring the head here. "

"There's no reception where they are. I made sure of that. I'd say we've got an impasse. If we turn up mob handed they'll be gone before we're near, if you turn up without me the same, you've got to take a risk."

"Alright, but my men will follow. I don't trust you Johnson, I never have. And don't forget, the girl stays here." then to Maria, "You know what to do if I don't return."

Maria nodded and smiled in acknowledgement.

Johnson sat at a kitchen table. One of his accomplices brewed coffee. He gave Johnson a cup, which he sipped thoughtfully. The door opened and the second henchman came in with a metal box that still had clods of earth stuck to it. He placed it on the table.

"Right, get down to the boat, make sure it's all ready then call me. If there are any problems let me know immediately. We'll make a run for Turkey. It's not ideal but we need to get off the island now while Marcos is distracted."

The man nodded and left.

"What do we do now?" The other man asked.

"We wait." Johnson replied.

CHAPTER 6

As Hunter and Marcos left dawn was breaking, the sky lightening from black to a more translucent blue; the stars that had shone so brightly in the dark of the night were now few and far between. The air was fresh and there wasn't a cloud in the sky, it was going to be another beautiful day and, Hunter thought, "a decisive one."

"You drive!" Marcos ordered and threw Hunter the car keys. Then pointed with his revolver to the white Mercedes saloon that was parked under a wooden structure covered with reed to shield the car from the heat of the sun. Hunter unlocked the car and got into the driver's seat. He adjusted the seat and the rear view mirror as Marcos got in. The car started first time and Hunter pulled off and out onto the road. He drove at a steady pace, and a glance in the rear view mirror showed him that Marcos's men were following close behind.

The car hit a pothole sending a shudder throughout the bodywork bouncing Marcos in his seat.

"Careful, I wouldn't want my finger to slip on the trigger." Marcos said with a grin.

Hunter was only to well aware of the proximity of the gun and his ribs.

"If you did you wouldn't get the head would you?" Hunter said trying to make light of the situation.

"But you'd get the girl.... in heaven." Marcos said laughing at his own joke.

Hunter sensed a slight opportunity to gain a small advantage. "You think I care about her?" He asked with a sneer.

"Ah, your true colours are coming out." Marcos laughed.

"Think about it," said Hunter, "your insurance policy is null and void, if you kill her, it won't bother me but it will be trouble for you."

Marcos looked more serious. "Luckily I have another policy and it's right behind me."

"For the moment." Hunter thought, then said to Marcos, "You've got all the bases covered, haven't you?"

"You know me well enough, I don't like to leave things to chance." Marcos said confidently.

There was a pause in the conversation; Hunter reduced the speed of the car subtly. The longer the journey lasted, the longer Hunter had to work out a plan of action, he was formulating one as he drove, it was sketchy and it depended on Johnson and a stroke of luck but at that moment he saw the opportunity he was waiting for, ahead was a queue of half a dozen cars behind a petrol tanker moving slowly up hill toward a blind bend. Hunter gently accelerated and unnoticed by Marcos opened up a gap between himself and the following car. As they came up behind the queue Hunter made his move, he dropped the car down two gears and floored the accelerator, the nose of the car lifted and the engine revs immediately climbed to the red line the engine banging on the rev limiter, the automatic gearbox wanting to change up, but Hunter held it down in second. The burst of acceleration took them up and past the first car in the queue as Hunter pulled out onto the outside.

"What are you doing!" Marcos shouted. "There's no room, pull in!"

Hunter kept the accelerator pinned to the floor, inside he was praying that there wasn't another lorry coming in the opposite direction, this was it, he was level with the tanker on the inside of the bend. Behind Marco's men had caught up with the queue but held back the driver not wanting to risk overtaking on the blind bend. Hunter kept going, Marcos screaming at him to stop, but they were committed. Luck was on Hunter's side, he was level with the front of the tanker as the bend unwound and he saw a delivery truck coming in the opposite direction. Hunter pulled in just missing the tanker and fish tailing down the road as he desperately worked at the steering wheel in an attempt to keep the car on the road and avoid hitting an embankment on one side or plummeting down an unprotected drop that fell to the sea on the other, his actions were accompanied by the blaring horn of the tanker whose driver slammed on the brakes and in so doing lost control. The driver valiantly fought to keep the lorry straight on the road but the momentum of the trailer continued, overtaking the cab and jack knifing the lorry. When it stopped, the cab was facing forward with the trailer completely blocking the road its rear wheels half over the precipice.

Marcos looked around over his shoulder and instantly realised he had lost his cover, "stop now!" he ordered.

"I don't think so," Hunter said. "We're making such good progress."

"I should shoot you now."

"Good plan," Hunter replied, all of a sudden he was enjoying himself, feeling he at last had the upper hand, "shoot me, you'll never find the head and I'll make sure you come over the edge with me."

Marcos looked around again, then turned back round to Hunter and smiled. "It really is you. I was convinced until I heard you talk, your voice seemed different, but something about the girl and her story persuaded me that it was you, but I still wasn't sure until now. Come on why don't we forget what happened, we had the potential to make a lot of money together but individually it doesn't work. What do you say?" With which Marcos put down the gun and held out his hand for Hunter to shake.

Hunter looked at Marcos with what he hoped was a knowing grin. "You don't change do you? Put your hand down and keep facing forward."

"Suit yourself." Marcos said and did as he was requested.

It was at this point Hunter had an idea, he slowed the car and pulled in at a lay-by. "I know you like secrecy," Hunter said, "so just to repay the complement I want you to get in the back of the car and cover your head."

Marcos laughed. "You're forgetting who's got the gun." Marcos said.

"And you're forgetting who's got the head." Hunter retorted. "We can sit here all day, or I can take you on a tour of the island, or you can do as I ask and we can go straight to the goods."

Marcos shrugged, "what the hell, but I'll have the gun pointing at you all the way."

"Looks like we've got a deal." Hunter said.

Marcos got out of the car and into the back. He laid down on the back seat and covered his head with his jacket, "I feel ridiculous." He said.

"Don't worry it's a short journey." Hunter said, then started the car and pulled back out onto the road. Ten minutes later they were outside Johnson's place. Hunter drove in very slowly trying to make as little sound as possible. He parked blocking in the one car that was still in the driveway.

Hunter got out of the car and Marcos sat up taking the jacket off his head. Hunter opened the rear passenger door for Marcos who got out and followed Hunter around to the back door of the house. Hunter tried it; it was unlocked and opened straight into the kitchen. Johnson's assistant was alone at the table, he looked up, "Why have you come 'round there he asked." Then he saw Marcos behind Hunter. "What's he doing there?" the man asked, then in a double take, "You're the other guy!"

"The other guy?" Marcos exclaimed. Then pushed Hunter to one side and covered both of them with his gun, he turned to the man at the table. "Are you trying to tell me there's two of them?" The man nodded.

Then Marcos laughed. "Oh you had me going there for a moment." Then to Hunter, "You've trained them well." Then he pointed at the steel box on the table. "Is that it."

"Don't ask me." Hunter said. "I'm not Johnson."

"Shut up!" Marcos barked, "don't start all that again!" Then to the man, "open it!"

The man leant forward and unlatched the lid of the box.

"Over there." Marcos pointed with his gun to the corner where Hunter was standing. The man complied then Marcos moved forward to the table and looked into the box. For a moment he was completely absorbed in what he was looking at, then a noise broke his concentration he looked around and saw Johnson pointing his automatic at him, his assistant pointing his gun at Hunter.

"What the hell!" Marcos exclaimed.

"Yes it's uncanny isn't it? He had you fooled didn't he? It was lucky for me he turned up when he did. Unfortunately you didn't hold on to him. If you had I would have been away and you'd never have suspected. He gave me the slip but now he's come through again, by bringing you to me I can kill two birds with one stone, or rather two bullets, and no one will suspect. It will look like a squabble between two crooks that ended badly. It couldn't be better."

"If I hadn't seen it for myself I would never have believed it. You must have been separated at birth." Marcos said.

"You'll never know, now put your gun on the table and sit down!"

Marcos complied and sat behind the table facing the door.

"You stay over there by the door." Johnson said pointing at Hunter.

Hunter moved back to the door still covered by Johnson's assistant as Johnson took Marcos's gun from the table.

"That's right, now let's see, you surprised Marcos, and you both shot simultaneously, it's a bit far fetched but it should work, unfortunately for both of you they were fatal."

"Hold on." Hunter interrupted, "Marcos, call Maria and let Kate go, she's no use to you now."

Marcos was confused, "I thought there was no signal?"

Hunter was exasperated, "How do I know? I'm Hunter remember?"

"She won't be any use at all when Maria's finished with her." Johnson interrupted.

"You bastard!" Hunter exclaimed.

"Calm down." Johnson ordered. "It won't help you to get so excited, then again it doesn't really matter, you're dead any way." Johnson levelled the gun at Hunter.

"Besides she's seen our faces, we can't leave any loose ends." Marcos continued causing Johnson to laugh.

"You're wonderful, you've got seconds to live but you think you are still in charge. Maybe you should be saying your prayers instead."

"Murder was never your thing," Marcos replied, "come on Johnson, kill him, then you have your anonymity and we can work together again."

"You think I'd trust you?" Johnson sneered at Marcos "my only dilemma now is which one of you to kill first."

"But Johnson..." Marcos started to plead as Johnson moved around behind him and crouched down so that he would be shooting from Marcos sitting level.

While they had been arguing Johnson's man had not been paying attention to Hunter who had let the door off the latch, "it's now or never!" he thought and was out the door in a flash, slamming it behind him and running headlong out of the building and into the bright light of day the sound of gunshots ringing behind him, he glanced back and in so doing tripped landing heavily face first winding himself, he struggled to get back to his feet and as he did so he realised everything had gone eerily quiet.

He stood up gun in hand and faced the building. For a moment he was rooted to the spot not sure if in the next instant someone would come out and the nightmare would start again. Torn between his desire to get away from the scene, to get back and save Kate, and his curiosity to see what had happened he waited. No one came out and curiosity won, so Hunter made his way cautiously to the door. There was no sound from inside so he stood to the side of the door and kicked it open. The sight that greeted him was one he could never have imagined outside a Hollywood movie. The walls were sprayed red and Johnson's assistant lay on the floor in a congealing pool of blood, Hunter didn't need to check to know he was dead. Johnson lay on the floor behind Marcos a bloodstain growing on his shirt, dead as well, Marcos though was still alive sprawled over the table, his hands clutching the metal box, his back covered in blood half blown away by the exit wounds of the shots he had received, panting, close to death.

"What is Maria going to do?" Hunter demanded.

Marcos did not reply, either he didn't hear or could not or would not talk.

"Come on, you've had it, don't let an innocent person die as well."

With a huge effort Marcos raised his head stared straight at Hunter and forced a blooded grin, "I'll see you in hell." He gasped out, then his head dropped and the panting stopped.

"NO!" Hunter let out a howl. "No! No! No!" He raised his hands to his head, he was distraught. He started to weep, shaking uncontrollably. He turned and paced up and down the room, trying to regain control. He went to the sink and ran the tap, taking a long drink of water then splashing his face. When he had finished he had regained some semblance of control. He took a deep breath and summoned his internal strength. He'd saved himself now he needed to save Kate.

"Come on Hunter," he said to himself, "You haven't got much time."

Hunter picked up the dead man's revolver took out the magazine and removed the remaining few bullets. He picked up Johnson's automatic, removed the magazine and reloaded it, luckily the rounds were the same calibre, he re-inserted the magazine, checked that the safety catch was on and stuck it in the front of his trousers. He turned to leave then paused at the doorway, he turned to once again face the gruesome scene then returned to the table. He lifted Marcos's hands from the box and picked it up, it was heavy and took some effort to carry out to the car but whatever was in it had caused him so much trouble he wasn't going to leave it behind. He put the box on the ground opened the boot of the car and put the box in. He got into the car started it and pulled away from the building, hoping that he would never return and never witness a scene like that again.

He had to get back to Marcos's place as soon as possible, he could remember the route and set off as fast as he could. He sped down the coast road, overtaking slower traffic wherever possible. He passed the point where the jack knifed lorry was being pulled back onto the road and waited trying to look inconspicuous as the police guided the traffic through a temporary contraflow. Once past the obstruction he picked up speed again and was soon approaching Marcos's place. He slowed down and tried to gather his thoughts. "What was he going to do?" He assumed that Marcos's men would have returned there, he also assumed that they were armed. He pulled over and paused to work out a plan of attack but he could not think logically, his mind was occupied with thoughts of what might be happening to Kate. Then he remembered something that he had read, which was that the last thing a stronger force expects is for you to attack and that if you do so they will be so surprised that for a short time you will have the upper hand. So that was his plan, straight in and hopefully straight out again but this time with Kate. He pulled the gun from the waist of his trousers and put it on his lap, then he paused. He looked at the gun and wondered, "could he actually pull the trigger and shoot someone? Would he just freeze into inaction?" He didn't know, after all he was used to settling disputes by civilised dialogue not violent action but then before today he'd never punched anyway in anger of clobbered someone with a stick. He looked up and out of the car unfocused apparently staring straight into the distance but in reality looking deep into his soul. Then he pulled away and drove straight into the entrance to Marcos's place.

There was only one other car outside which he recognised as the one that Marcos's henchmen had been driving when they were following him earlier, so he assumed that they at least were there and he hoped that Kate was still there as well. He pulled up parallel to the door and in an instant was out of the car, gun in hand, safety catch off. He kicked the door with all the force he could muster and to his surprise it swang open, he burst through, "Kate!" he shouted as loudly as he could then fired a shot into the ceiling immediately wishing he hadn't as in such a small space the crack of the round was almost deafening. It had done the trick though, Marcos's men, Xenephon and Alexandros, burst into the hallway in front of him stopping at the sight of the automatic that Hunter had trained on them. Now was not the time for indecision so Hunter followed what he had seen and heard many times in the movies.

"Hands up!" he ordered raising his free hand above his head to show them what it was he wanted them to do. They followed his actions. Then Hunter stepped forward keeping his eyes and his gun trained on the two men and patted them down. He pulled a revolver from Xenephon's waistband, checked the safety was on and stuck it in the waistband of his trousers, before checking over Alexandros who was unarmed. "Where's Kate!" Neither of the men answered, and in truth Hunter knew she wasn't there but he had to check. He herded the two men in front of him as they went on a tour of the building, finding every room empty and ending up in the kitchen. Hunter gestured to the men to move two chairs back to back and sit down, which they did, then looked around for something to secure them with. He felt he needed to restrain them somehow, but with only one free hand and having to keep them covered with the gun he wasn't likely to be able to tie them up even of by some chance there was a convenient rope lying around. Then he noticed a large roll of parcel tape on the counter. "It might just work." He thought to himself.

Round and round Hunter went wrapping the two men together and to their chairs until the roll of tape was completely used up. The men were then tightly restrained, taped to each other and to the chairs. They might break out, but it would take time and effort. Hunter was rather smugly self satisfied with what he had done but he stopped himself from excessive self-congratulation as the reality of the situation and why he was there came back to him.

"Where is Kate!" He demanded.

Both men sat impassively looking straight ahead in their opposite directions.

"Look it's over, Marcos is dead."

That got a reaction, both men looked around in surprise before quickly resuming their their dumb stares.

"At the moment you are accessories only to, well I don't know what, but as far as I do know you are not yet guilty of murder. If that woman kills Kate and you don't do anything to help me stop it you'll be as guilty as she is. Come on tell me where they've gone, it's all over, do yourselves a favour." He couldn't be sure if he was getting through or even how much English the men understood, he paused to let his words settle in. "Why let an innocent person die? For what? Marcos is dead, Johnson's dead, I've got the head.." Hunter broke off as Xenophon looked around at him.

"You have the head?"

"Yes."

"And Marcos is really dead?"

"Yes."

"You're telling the truth?"

"Of course I'm telling the truth. Where's your phone? Call Maria off!"

"She will only answer to Marcos, did you bring his phone?"

Hunter cursed himself, he hadn't thought to take Marcos's phone. "Then tell me where she's taken Kate! I need to know where Kate is and I need to know now!"

Xenophon smiled a little smile, "Then release us and give us the head. Then we'll tell you where they've gone."

Hunter had to think this through, but quickly, he played for time, time that he didn't really have but needed. He had to get it right.

"I can't do that, besides which I'm the one holding the gun." He waggled the gun at Xenophon who just sneered back.

"You want the girl, we want the head, it's a straight swap."

Hunter had it. "You're right I don't care about the head, but if I release you, you'll just as likely follow me and I won't get either. Here's what I'll do. I'll get the head and leave it in here, and I'll give you a knife to cut yourselves free, by the time you've done that I'll be long gone and there will be no point in you following me."

Xenephon thought for a moment, "get the head, let us see it."

Hunter knew he was at a disadvantage, the other men knew he wasn't a killer and wouldn't use the gun, he didn't care about the head and they didn't care about Kate, but he realised that he did have some leverage, they did care about the head and they did care about their freedom. He had to use that knowledge to help him rescue Kate because he was in no doubt that Maria was a psychopath and would have no compulsion in killing her.

"Don't try anything while I'm gone." He said, realising the emptiness of the implied threat as the words left his mouth.

He hurried out to the car, took the metal box from the boot, and returned as quickly as he could. To his surprise the men appeared not to have moved while he had been gone. He placed the box at their feet, checked that they were still securely bound then opened the box lid.

The men looked into the box and their faces lit up with the satisfaction of greed. Xenephon looked back up at Hunter, "Now the knife."

"Where are they?"

Xenephon gestured with a turn of the head to an obvious rack of knives hanging on the wall by the cooker. Hunter checked then all for sharpness before picking out the bluntest. He placed the knife on the table away from the men, "Right, you've got the head, there's the knife, you can shuffle over to it, now where have they gone?"

"To the southern tip of the island, as far away from anyone as they can get. There's a dirt track leads down to a beach and some old fisherman's buildings, they'll be there."

"What's it called?"

"It doesn't have a name, but it is just near Prasonisis."

From the way Xenephon spoke, Hunter didn't believe a word. He was being sent on a wild goose chase all the way down to the far end of the island while Xenephon and Alexandros would make their escape while Kate suffered at the hands of Maria. He pulled Xenephon's revolver from his waist belt, cocked it and flicked off the safety catch. As he did so he could see Xenephon tighten his muscles and his expression subtly change from one of confidence to uncertainty. Hunter held the gun pointing up toward the ceiling and paced from one side of the kitchen to the other, then he stopped and looked directly at Xenephon.

"You're lying! Tell me the truth or I will not be responsible for my actions."

Xenephon did not reply.

"For Christ's sake what does it matter?" With which he fired a shot into the floor between Xenephons legs. Xenephon looked down in shock and Hunter noticed that he was starting to sweat, beads forming around his hairline, one trickling down his cheek. Alexandros gabbled in Greek which brought him what Hunter assumed was a sharp rebuke. Hunter was winning he had to press home the advantage and he saw Alexandros as the weak point. He moved to stand in front of him. If Xenephon had looked worried, it was nothing, Alexandros was sweating his face contorted with fear. He hadn't been able to see Hunter before and probably didn't understand English, he must have been sitting wondering listening to the words and the sounds before being shocked by the gunshot. Hunter was sure he would break.

"I'm not used to guns, that was a lucky shot, I don't know where the next one will go." He levelled the gun pointing it straight at Alexandros genitals. "You didn't want children did you?" He asked with what he hoped was a cruel smile.

"Monolithos.. Monolithios!" ....Alexandros shouted. Xenephon writhed in a vain attempt to free himself and shouted at Alexandros, what, Hunter didn't know but he could imagine.

He slipped the safety catch back and shoved the gun back in his waistband. "Thank you, that's all I needed to know." Then he turned to leave stopping at the door he returned to the knife rack and took down all the sharp knives. He picked the knife off the table and threw them all into the box with the head. "Deal's off, you should have told me the truth." Then he picked up the box and made his way out to the car.

Hunter put the box back in the boot of the car then got in. He opened the glove box, then checked in the door storage. He sat up straight and hit the steering wheel. "No map!" He exclaimed with irritation. "Right." He started the car and drove back the way he had come, then headed south down the coast road. After a short time he saw a petrol station up ahead. It was quite modern, the pumps shaded by a large roof which joined a shop come pay-booth. Hunter slowed down and pulled in stopping in a parking space in front of the shop. He put both guns in the glove box before he quickly got out of the car and dashed in, to be greeted by the ice cool of an efficient air conditioning system which made the perspiration on his body suddenly feel cold and dry. Musak filled the air and behind the pay counter sat a bored looking man who watched Hunter as he made his way past the aisles of snacks and cold drinks straight for a rotary display which held a few maps and guidebooks. Hunter grabbed a map and went to leave, pausing at the door he felt in his pocket but there was nothing there.

"I'm sorry I haven't got any money but it's a matter of life and death." Hunter blurted out.

The attendant stared back at him impassively.

"I haven't got time for this." Hunter mumbled under his breath and dashed back into the heat of the day and got into the car. He fired it up and drove off back onto the coast road.

The attendant had watched him without registering a flicker of emotion and as Hunter disappeared up the road he picked up the telephone and dialled.

Hunter had the map open on the passenger seat as he drove as fast as he could. Glancing down at the map he didn't notice that a lorry that had been, he thought, far in the distance was moving extremely slowly. Hunter glanced back up and saw the rear of the lorry filling his view ahead, a shot of adrenaline surged through his body as he slammed on the brakes and just managed to slow down before making impact. He dropped back a few car lengths then darted out to see past the lorry just as a platoon of cars passed in the other direction. He pulled back in, cursing to himself and dropped back a little further. He looked out again. This time it was clear so he dropped a gear and floored the accelerator speeding past the lorry in one long burst of acceleration. The road ahead was clear so Hunter kept it nailed, the lorry disappearing rapidly behind him.

Soon after, the road started to wind up a steep hill. Hunter attacked the road as if he was driving a rally stage, sliding the car round the bends accelerating hard on the short straights before dabbing the brakes and accelerating through the next bend. He was working hard, sweating in the heat, his senses heightened, if he'd had time to think about it he would have really enjoyed himself, however the only thought on his mind was to get to where he was going as quickly as possible.

The road levelled out and Hunter slowed down as he entered a small village. He kept his speed down as he passed through, but failed to notice the police car idling in the shade of a narrow side street. The road turned as it left the village and as Hunter accelerated away he also failed to see the police car pull out of the side road and follow in his direction. In fact Hunter didn't even notice that he was being followed until he heard the siren and saw the blue lights of the rapidly closing police car reflected in his rear view mirror.

"Bugger!" Hunter exclaimed to himself and tried to go even faster. He quickly pulled out a small lead before rounding the next bend just as a shepherd was leading his flock out of a field onto the road. Hunter braked hard and hit the horn, the sudden blare scattering the sheep and leaving Hunter enough room to pass.

It was different for the pursuing police, as they came round the bend the road was full of bleating sheep and one irate shepherd trying to get them under control. The police men waved and shouted out of the window to try and clear the road but had to move at walking pace to get through the flock, by which time Hunter had turned off the main road and was heading down a rough side road toward the sea.

Up to his left Hunter could see an ancient ruined castle. He stopped by a side turn and checked the map. He turned off and headed slowly toward the castle up a narrow road that ended at a dusty parking area. Hunter pulled up next to the only other car there a car that he recognised, a car that he'd first seen three days previously and in which he'd had the misfortune to be kidnapped, the car that was driven by Maria. Hunter opened the glove box and took out the automatic, he got out of the car and thrust the gun into the back of his trousers. He looked up toward the castle and scanned around but he could see nothing moving, so he headed up the path toward the castle walls. Once he reached them he proceeded cautiously into the castle. Inside there was no roof save the sky and no movement except a cool sea breeze. He looked 'round but there was nothing. He made his way up a flight of stone steps to the ramparts and looked around at the sea and the surrounding countryside, and then saw, down on the cliff top, what he had been looking for. Two women, one blonde one brunette. He hurriedly made his way back down and out of the castle. Skirting the walls on the land ward side he made his way round to where he had seen the women. They came into view fifty yards in front of him, Kate her back to the sea Maria with her back to Hunter. Neither saw him and he made his way toward them then stopped. Maria had a gun levelled at Kate's stomach. Hunter pulled out his revolver and let off the safety catch. With the gun trained on Maria he shouted out. "Stop!" The drama of their situation interrupted, Kate and Maria both looked at him, Kate with hope Maria with hate.

"Where is Marcos?" She demanded.

"He's dead." Hunter replied coldly. "It's over let her go."

Maria thought for a moment. "You killed him?" She asked.

"No Johnson did." Hunter replied.

"But you're Johnson." Maria exclaimed, confused.

"Not that again! I'm not Johnson, Johnson is dead."

"Don't take me for a complete fool." Maria spat out, "You've killed Marcos now I'll kill you and then I'll kill the girl." She raised her gun aiming at Hunter.

"Wait, Hunter shouted. "I've got the head in the car, it's yours just let Kate go."

"Liar!" Maria screamed and as she pulled the trigger of her gun Hunter fell flat on the ground. But there was no crack, no echoing report, no lead projectile whistling past Hunter's head, instead there was just a click. Maria looked at the gun and pulled back the mechanism to bring another round into the firing chamber. As she did so Kate grabbed her arm pulling it back with such force that Maria dropped the gun. Maria swung her free arm catching Kate square on the cheek causing her to let go. They struggled trying to grab each other, moving closer to the cliff edge and in their impromptu dance their positions changed again and again until Maria her back to the sea slipped, the cliff edge having suddenly given way beneath her. In her fall she managed to grab Kate's arm and pull her to the ground. There they lay panting with the exertion of the struggle Maria holding Kate's arm with a vice like grip as she hung half over the edge of the cliff, hanging on to Kate for all her life was worth, while Kate all the time was gradually sliding down with her. They stared into each other's eyes, Maria's full of arrogance, hate and loathing, Kate's full of tears, fear and pity. "If I go you're coming with me." Maria spat out.

Kate didn't want to die, Not there not then and not with this evil woman. She tried to shake her arm free but Maria's grip was too tight. They continued to slide until only Maria's head and shoulders were above the cliff top the rest of her body hung free in space and Kate felt Maria's weight would pull her arm out the socket.

Hunter who had got to his feet as soon as the fight had started fell on Kate, one arm over her shoulder the other held her forearm relieving the pressure on her other shoulder, his extra weight keeping her from going over the edge. There they stayed, no one able to move, Maria hanging in space from Kate's arm, Hunter holding onto Kate preventing her going over, then Kate having freed her spare arm summoned all the force she could muster and punched Maria straight in the face. The blow was too much for her the shock of the impact forced her to involuntarily release her grip and she fell, free falling down to crash on to the rocks below, watched all the way by a stunned Kate. Hunter pulled Kate back from the edge and still holding onto her looked over. Maria's body lay in a bizarre contorted position on the boulders, her hair moving with the ebb and flow of the water like dark black strands of seaweed, a dark slick of blood flowing away from her body. Hunter looked back up to Kate who was sobbing uncontrollably, he helped her to her feet and kept holding her as they moved away from the cliff edge.

"I've never seen anybody die before." Kate sobbed.

"Neither had I" Hunter replied "and I hope I never have to again."

They sat down a safe way back from the cliff edge still holding onto each other looking out to sea.

"What happened to you?" Kate asked through her tears.

"It was pretty horrible," Hunter replied, "I got here as soon as I could."

"I'm glad you did." Kate said resting her head on Hunter's

shoulder. Hunter looked down at her and despite her bruised cheek and roughed up appearance thought he had never seen any one as beautiful in his life. Kate looked up wide-eyed and they kissed.

When they broke off Kate leant her head back down on Hunter's shoulder. "What are we going to do now?" She asked.

Hunter looked out at the sea. "Go to the police, tell the whole story, return the head and hope they believe us."

"The head, I'd almost forgotten. I've been dreaming of seeing it, finding out what it is, but now, after it's caused so much trouble, and a death, I just don't know."

"I haven't told you but it's more than one death."

"Oh my god, I didn't know. Who else?"

"Marcos, Johnson, another man, I don't know who he is, but they all killed each other. It was a shocking scene."

"And all for money, how pointless."

Kate looked away out to the sea, Hunter followed her gaze and for a few moments they were separated by their individual thoughts. Then Kate stood up, she took Hunter's hand and pulled him to his feet. "Come on, We'd better get on with it, besides I need to see this thing."

They started walking back to the parking space leaving the cliff and Maria's open briney grave behind them.

"You know, we'd better get our story straight about this." Hunter said.

Kate looked at him questioningly.

"I'm suggesting that we don't tell the police that you punched her, I mean it's totally justifiable under the circumstances, but I just think it's better to agree not to mention it. As far as anyone is concerned she just couldn't hold on any longer."

"I don't want to lie."

"We won't be lying, we'll just leave out that one detail."

"What if someone saw us?"

"If they did they'd be so far away they could never be sure, besides, eye witness evidence is never that reliable, I'm just saying to avoid complications it's better to brush over that aspect of what happened. Are we agreed?"

Kate nodded, "I suppose so."

"And don't elaborate, she was hanging onto your arm, you were trying to prevent yourself being pulled over, all of which is true, then she let go which is also true. Keep it simple like that and I'll say the same."

"I don't know, my conscience says I should tell the whole truth, what if they put me under oath?"

Hunter stopped and turned to Kate. "Conscience? Do you think she had a conscience? Did any of them? They were motivated by greed, and in her case some other weird turn on. If it was you who had gone over the edge they wouldn't have had any conscience about it. So just keep it simple and you'll be fine."

Again Kate nodded, "yes I guess you're right." They continued walking toward the car park. "What do you think would happen if I did tell them about the punch?"

"I don't know Greek law, maybe nothing, maybe a manslaughter charge, whatever it's best not to let that possibility arise."

They continued in silence each with their own thoughts until they reached the car. They paused for a moment before Hunter opened the boot, then they both looked in at the box neither wanting to immediately open it.

"I'm a bit nervous." Kate said,

"Why?"

"What if it's a disappointment? After all that's happened, four people have died for this, I'm not sure I do want to see it."

Hunter squeezed Kate's hand. "Don't worry I'm sure you won't be disappointed." Then he opened the box. He took the knives out and placed them on the boot floor then pulled the material that covered the head to one side.

Kate stared into the box, goggle-eyed. Eventually she spoke. "It's incredible, I've never seen such a perfectly preserved artefact from this period."

"It's valuable then?" Hunter asked.

"Priceless," Kate spoke very softly, "But it can't be sold, it has to be kept for everyone to see."

"I never thought of anything else." Hunter said with a smile then turned as he heard a car come into the car park. "Take a good look now, you may not see it again for a while."

"What..." Kate looked up and saw the Police getting out of the car. "Oh I see, I guess we don't have to go to them now."

The two Policemen had their guns drawn and were aiming them at Hunter taking cover behind the doors of the Police car. They shouted and Hunter realised he was still holding the automatic. He put his free hand in the air and very carefully laid the gun down on the ground, then raised his other hand, Kate had also raised her hands and they both edged back.

"Tell them there's another one in the glove box of the car." Hunter ordered.

Kate shouted out to the police and one of them picked up the first gun using his pen and slipped it into a plastic bag before taking the revolver from the glove box and repeating the action. He returned to the police car while the other searched both Hunter and Kate and finding nothing they relaxed and holstered their weapons.

CHAPTER 7

Kate tried to explain to the police what had happened, but as soon as she told them that Maria had gone over the cliff they stopped her. One of the officers went down to the cliff edge while his colleague radioed back to the main police station in Rhodes town. They waited for the officer to return from the cliff top, he wasn't long and returned with a shake of the head. Maria's body was not to be seen, it had either sunk or drifted out to sea. There was a brief conversation between the policemen who concluded that they shouldn't do anything until a more senior officer arrived, so they separated Kate and Hunter, and allowed them to sit in the shade of the Castle ramparts while they waited. Hunter lay down and drifted in to a light sleep, his mind retracing the events of the previous days since he had arrived. The image of carnage at Johnson's kept popping up but each time was replaced by that of Kate on the beach the first time he had met her two days previously. It was an image he wanted to hang onto but in turn was replaced by questions. Who was the old man at Lindos? How had he known Hunter would be there? Had Xenephon and Alexandros got away? Why hadn't the Police been interested in his story? His mind went round in circles trying to square the events and answer his own questions but it was hopeless.

Kate in the meantime was tense, before Hunter's suggestion that she didn't talk about the punch it hadn't, in all the excitement, occurred to her that there was the least possibility that she could be guilty of anything. "Wasn't she the victim?" After all, she'd been kidnapped, tortured and would quite likely have been murdered if Hunter hadn't turned up when he did.

She wondered how she had become mixed up in such awful events, she looked over at Hunter who was lying down with his eyes closed and wondered what it was about this man that had drawn her to him. Immediately she answered her own question, she trusted him.

As she waited Kate was haunted by the sight of Maria's body being washed on and off the rocks by the swell, her eyes open her mouth contorted in a twisted smile, it was an image that she did not want in her head, but one that was hard to shift.

An hour later a convoy of vehicles arrived. A young detective took control as the uniformed officers cordoned off the site. Kate lead him down to the cliff top and showed him where Maria had fallen and explained what had happened that morning. When she had finished, they returned to the car park and Hunter was lead down to the cliff top to give his version of events. By the time he had finished another police officer had recovered Maria's gun and a patrol boat was below them slowly going back and forth, looking for Maria's body. A helicopter passed over head and started to circle, each rotation becoming wider as the search area expanded.

By that time Kate had been put in a police car and was on the way back to Rhodes town. The Head had been taken under armed guard to be locked up in it's own cell and messages had gone to Athens to summon the head of the Archaeological Crime Department and specialist forensic officers.

Hunter was put into a police car with the lead detective and accompanied by another two cars full of officers; he guided them to Johnson's house where the detective took a quick look inside and returned to the car visibly shocked. He issued orders to the uniformed officers and got back in the car leaving them to guard the building as Hunter led them to Marcos place. The detective went in with another two officers but was not there for long, Xenephon and Alexandros must have managed to free themselves and make their escape. The two uniformed officers remained while the detective drove back with Hunter to the main police station in Rhodes town.

Once at the police station Hunter was photographed and fingerprinted, then he gave a DNA sample before he was allowed to have a shower. He was given a pair of boxer shorts, a set of cotton overalls and some slippers to wear, his own cloths being taken away so that the forensic team could take more samples and imprints of his shoes. Once he was showered he was taken to a cell to await questioning. The cell was plain, a hard tiled floor, the walls and ceiling painted grey, a barred window above eye height, there was no furniture save a plastic chamber pot and a built in bunk which had a thin hard mattress, a blanket and a pillow. Behind him the heavy steel door was closed and locked and Hunter was left to contemplate what had happened and what the consequences may be. He thought through what had happened and tried to view the events from the point of view of an investigator. First he considered what crime he may be guilty of, or charged with. There were certainly traffic offences, but it was clear that although he was present he was not responsible for any of the deaths, and he had recovered the stolen head and been completely co-operative with the police showing them to Johnson's place and telling them everything he knew. He was confident the whole situation would soon be sorted out and he would be released, but even so, something nagged at the back of his mind.

His thoughts were soon interrupted when he was brought a tray of food and a bottle of water. He hadn't realised how hungry he was and devoured the bread and musaka that he had been given. He lay back on his bunk and sipping the water waited for the next act.

Later that day he was visited by a lawyer. He was a young man who was immaculately dressed in a well cut, hand stitched dark blue business suit, complemented by a spotless white shirt and patterned red tie. Hunter noticed that the lawyer's shoes were polished to a gleaming shine and that, although he looked as though he would have a heavy beard, he appeared to have just shaved and had a haircut. His judgement was spot on as that was exactly what Christos the lawyer had done. When he had got the call to come and represent an American tourist who was involved in a case of multiple deaths, organised crime and the smuggling of ancient antiquities he had felt the hairs on the back of his neck stand up. This could potentially be a big case and the opportunity for him to make a name for himself. He wanted to do it right and he felt that appearing immaculate would give him a certain gravitas when dealing with the investigating judge and the police, not to mention looking well if the case ended up in the press or on television.

"Good morning, I'm Christos Skouras, I've been appointed by the investigating judge to represent you as you are an alien and do not have representation here."

Hunter noted that Christos English was very good, even his accent, but like all non native speakers there were tell tales in his pronunciation that gave away the fact that English was not his first language. Hunter proffered his hand and they shook. "I'm hoping this will all be sorted out soon, by the way your English is excellent, where did you study?"

"I'll do my best for you Mr Hunter..."

"Call me John!" Hunter interrupted,

"As I said I'll do my best, John, and thank you for the complement, I learnt English here but from an English man, anyway I'm going to take you to an interview room where we can talk more comfortably."

Christos led Hunter out of the cell and they were accompanied down the corridor by the guard who waited outside as they went into an interview room. The room like the cell had only one window, at the top of a wall, which was made of opaque glass, was barred, and through which bright sunlight was diffused as it entered the room. The room had the same floor tiles as the cell and was painted the same grey but was furnished with a table and a number of chairs. Christos Took off his jacket and hung it on the back of the chair while Hunter sat down opposite him, then sat down himself and took a notepad and pen from his briefcase. He looked up and smiled. "How much do you know about the Greek legal system?"

Hunter shrugged, "a little about commercial law."

"But nothing about Criminal law?"

Hunter shook his head, "I'm not a criminal."

Christos smiled again, "I'm not suggesting you are, but we are dealing with the criminal law."

Hunter nodded in acquiescence.

"The system here is different to that in the U S or in Britain. The case is investigated by an Investigating Judge who is separate from the police, it is his duty to gather all the evidence whether it supports the case against you or it is in your favour. He will then take this information to the prosecutor. If the case is going to go to trial it is likely that you will be held in custody until that date..."

"Hold on, Hunter interrupted, I haven't been accused of anything, I haven't been charged with anything, I've come here voluntarily I'm an innocent person who has been mistaken for someone else. I'm the victim. I'm trying to help the police sort out what has happened and more than that I've helped to recover some valuable ancient artefact. I should be praised and getting the red carpet treatment not waiting in cells and being given a run down on how long I'm likely to be detained!"

Christos let Hunter finish before he spoke in a measured tone. "Mr Hunter, John, I am on your side, but as far as the police are concerned you are involved with everything that has happened and as far as the law and the investigating judge are concerned you are a suspect and cannot be allowed to go before they have cleared you. You can be held almost indefinitely, and under our system you can be charged and then held while evidence is gathered and then released if there is no case to answer. I'm sorry but that's the way it works here, now you'd better tell me the whole story, and remember to tell me everything because you will be repeating it all again later."

Hunter accepted his fate, he had a good feeling about Christos, someone who was so immaculate about his appearance would be good with detail and it would be details that they had to get right. "Can we get some coffee? You'll need it, it's a long story."

Christos got up and spoke to the guard. A few minutes later a tray was brought in with a flask of coffee and two plastic cups. Hunter poured one for Christos and one for himself then lent back in his chair and started relating the story.

Christos took copious notes and interrupted only to clarify details. When Hunter had finished there was a pause as Christos scanned his notes. Then he looked up at Hunter. "It's quite an incredible story, but as far as I can tell you have little to worry about, you were not responsible for any of the deaths I am sure once the bodies have been examined and the forensic tests completed you will be released. Be patient, it could take a little time, as I said, the Investigating Judge has to gather all the evidence. The next thing that will happen is that you will be asked to give an official statement, I'll be there with you, and then we can apply for you to be released, although as I said before don't be surprised if you are detained until all the evidence has been gathered. One thing comes to mind though, did anyone see you and Johnson together at the same time?"

"Yes, well actually now I think of it only Johnson, his accomplice and Marcos and they are all dead, no hold on there was another man working for Johnson, he wasn't there when the shooting happened, he would have seen both of us."

"I see thank you." Christos tidied his papers and put them in his briefcase. "I've got your employers details and the police will have your passport, so we can easily establish that you are who you say you are."

Hunter nodded his acknowledgement, then they stood up and shook hands.

The guard took Hunter back to his cell which was now illuminated by artificial light, the sun having, by this time, set. Hunter lay down on the bunk, pulled the blanket over him and fell asleep. He was woken soon after by the guard who bought him another meal, which Hunter hungrily devoured. When he had finished he made himself as comfortable as possible and folding his arm across his eyes to block out the light, again drifted off to sleep.

That night Hunter didn't sleep well, he was disturbed by vivid dreams, the events of the past few days being distorted, lengthened, shortened and made surreal. Eventually he woke with a start, light was pouring in through the window, he felt terrible, as if he had hardly slept, so he lay there and wondered what would happen next. He hadn't yet been charged with anything, and remembering what Christos had said the previous day he didn't expect to, but how long would he be detained for and what would happen with his job, that is, if he had a job to go back to? He assumed the police had contacted his employers as they had taken their contact details, it wasn't going to go down well. He had a good reputation within the company, and he assumed they would be supportive but at the same time it was a commercial business and he couldn't expect them to keep his position open forever. Hunter stopped himself, worrying about what hadn't yet happened wouldn't help him. He would deal with the consequences at the time. Now he had to deal with the Investigating Judge, that should be no problem, he had nothing to hide but he must be in the right co-operative state of mind. He got out of the bunk and stretched, first rotating his head then his shoulders. He stretched up and reached as far into the air as he could until he was fully extended on tiptoe then returned to a resting position. He rotated his torso then with his hands on his hips and his knees bent leant forward holding the position and stretching his lower back. Then he repeated the action but with his legs straight and touched his toes. He stretched his thigh muscles by holding each leg in turn behind his back and pushing his hips forward. He started to feel awake and more alive, he sat on the floor and hooking his toes under the bunk did a few sit ups then finished off with some press ups. Now he felt energised and ready for a shower and some breakfast.

He didn't have long to wait, as the door opened and a different guard brought in a tray with some fresh rolls, fruit and most importantly strong black coffee. Hunter thanked him, a pointless exercise really but Hunter's manners hadn't deserted him, then he sat on the bed and enjoyed the breakfast. When he had finished he knocked on the door and the guard took the tray away then returned and took Hunter to the bathroom for a shower.

The guard gave him a towel and a mini safety razor then stood to one side and watched bored as Hunter first showered and then shaved. The razor was pretty hopeless so it wasn't the best shave but Hunter managed to avoid cutting himself. He now felt ready to face his inquisitor and hoped that he would not have to wait long. His hopes were fulfilled, as it was barely fifteen minutes before the guard came back and took Hunter to an office.

The room was furnished with a desk on which among the normal accoutrements stood a digital recorder. The window was not barred and Hunter was glad that the window was partly open letting in a flow of fresh air. There was a display cabinet mainly full of books and on the wall behind the desk a number of framed certificates that Hunter didn't bother to read. Christos was waiting with the detective who had brought Hunter in and a woman who Hunter hadn't seen before. He was ushered into a chair next to Christos where they sat facing the Detective and the woman across the desk. She was tall and thin, her hair was dark but Hunter assumed dyed as although she wore well applied make up it didn't disguise the deepening lines around her lips, the slight hint of a moustache and the crows feet that even behind her large glasses were visible around her eyes. These he took as a good sign, as, although she looked serious they were the tell tale of someone who at other times laughed a lot. He guessed that she must have been in her fifties but could have been older, he glanced at her hands, often the guide to someone's real age but they were tanned with short trimmed red varnished nails that matched the more subtle red of her lipstick and gave nothing away.

Hunter took all this in, in seconds, and as he did so the woman gave him a cursory look making a similar assessment and finding herself making a judgement that no Investigating Judge faced with a potential triple murderer should make for, unknown to Hunter, as far as she was concerned that was what he was.

"I am Aella Frangos and I have been appointed to this case as the Investigating Judge. I understand that Mr Skouras has already explained the way the legal system works in Greece, so this morning I want to take a statement from you, do not leave out any details, I want to know everything that happened. We will record what you say and have a transcript made that you can then check. Is that clear?"

Hunter nodded his assent then, once the detective had started the digital recorder, started to once again recount the whole long story. Both the investigating judge and the Detective listened attentively throughout and let Hunter tell the story without interruption. When he had finished the detective turned off the recorder.

"Thank you Mr Hunter, for giving such a full and comprehensive statement, and that is to your credit. As you will no doubt be aware we have been conducting a forensic investigation at the two houses where you took us. We've picked up the two men who worked for Marcos, they were easy to find, and are wrapping up the rest of their organisation. They have confirmed a lot of your story, but there is a problem."

Hunter couldn't imagine what this may be but he had worried that there would be something that the police were not happy about, as far as he was concerned he had done nothing wrong, but put in the position of the police he would have been suspicious as they were.

The detective continued. "This man Johnson. You say he looked identical to you?"

"Yes almost, there was a slight difference, but even I would have mistaken us, it was uncanny."

"And you told us that he died in the house with Marcos?"

Hunter tensed, he had seen Johnson's dead body in the carnage of the room. Why the question? Surely they had the body? "Yes but you must have recovered the body?"

"That, Mr Hunter is the problem. There were only two bodies. Marcos and another man who we haven't identified yet, but who certainly looked nothing like you."

Hunter was stunned. He had seen Johnson, covered in blood, he must have been dead, it was inconceivable that he could have been alive, but he hadn't checked. Maybe just maybe he hadn't been killed after all.

"I don't know what to say, I saw the body, as I've told you I took the box with the head and went back to Marcos's to try to find Kate you know the story I've been through it several times."

"Yes and you've been very consistent. Miss Adams confirms all the parts where she was present, but of course she wasn't there all the time, and," the detective paused for emphasis, "She doesn't know who you really are."

"But my employer can confirm who I am, you've got all my details, there can be no confusion surely? Johnson must have been alive after all and somehow got away before I took you there, I never checked to see if he was dead, I just assumed," then he calmed himself, "what exactly are you suggesting?"

At this point Aella raised her hand, she was ready to talk again. "We have no record of any Johnson, of course it's likely he travelled on a false passport, or even more likely that Johnson isn't his real name. But we do have a problem. Look at it this way. A man arrives on the island, he claims that there is a case of mistaken identity and he has been chased by a gang of criminals who are convinced he is someone else. He looks identical to this other man, a man who is in the process of smuggling antiquities and incredibly he meets a fellow American who just happens to live on the island and is an expert in Greek artefacts who immediately takes this stranger into her house and helps him evade his pursuers. It sounds incredible doesn't it?"

Hunter had to admit that it did, he could understand their suspicion, he didn't answer the question.

"Now it is just possible that what you have said is true, if we had Johnson's body, if we had any witnesses other than Miss Adams, the point is, no one who is still alive has ever seen you and Johnson together, there is no body or record of him ever existing, and I think that there never was another man. I think that Johnson is your alias that Miss Adams is working with you and that you've made up this whole story to cover your actions."

Hunter's mind raced, of course, Marcos and Johnson's man were the only ones who had ever seen them together and they were both dead. What the detective was postulating was entirely possible, in fact looking from the other side it seemed far more likely than the truth. Then he spoke. "I can see why you might think that, it all fits quite well but there are two things, Johnson had another man who wasn't there at the shoot out and the old man at Lindos, if you find him he knows that I am not Johnson..."

The detective interrupted him. "There was no old man. That's part of the story you made up. You've been laying a false trail and that is exactly what it is. All the people you've told us about, the hotel staff, the officer you saw here in Rhodes, the sailor on the tourist boat, the ticket seller at Kritinia, the garage attendant, they all confirm the facts, and Miss Adams movements are confirmed but none of that changes the facts that there are three people dead, we have witnesses who claim that you are Johnson and we do not have anyone else who fits your description. You're lying, you've been lying all along now tell the truth."

"I am telling the truth!" Hunter burst out. "This is absurd... surely the DNA will show that there was a third man in the house, his blood must have been everywhere, you've got mine surely that will prove there was a third man?"

The detective smiled, "Maybe, we'll just have to wait and see. Now is there anything you want to tell us!"

Hunter was calmer now, "No, I've told you everything, I have nothing to add."

"That's a shame," Aella said "it would save a lot of time and trouble if you just told us the truth now, anyway we are now going to officially charge you." She handed Christos a sheet of paper, which he read carefully.

"Are you happy that it is all in order Mr Skouras?"

Christos nodded his assent.

Aella looked directly at Hunter. "John Hunter I am charging you with three counts of murder, one of the theft of antiquities, and minor driving offences. Please sign the sheet to acknowledge that you understand the charges."

"But I'm innocent!" Hunter let out.

Christos interrupted and spoke calmly to Hunter, "It's a formality John, everyone is charged while a case is being investigated, sign the sheet."

Hunter reached forward and took the pen that was being proffered by the detective, then reluctantly signed the charge sheet. In turn Christos, Aella, and the detective also signed the sheet.

"Thank you." Aella said. "Unless you have any thing else to add you can return to your cell."

"Actually I'd like to consult with my client." Christos said.

"Very well the guard will take you to the interview room."

The detective issued an order to the guard who moved forward and stood by Hunter. "We'll call for you when we need you."

Hunter looked stunned, the way the law operated in Greece was quite different to what he was used to in the States. He suddenly realised that he was potentially looking at a long stay in prison unless the DNA evidence showed that there was another man present when Marcos had been killed. He just hoped that Kate would be released soon.

He tried hard to stay calm, and was about to protest again when he caught Christos's expression from the corner of his eye, he looked around at him and read the message in his expression that said "Not now." So Hunter metaphorically bit his tongue and followed Christos's lead as he stood up, thanked Aella and left the office. They were accompanied back to the interview room by the police officer who waited outside while Hunter and Christos went in.

"Well done," Christos started, "your statement was very clear, and just what you told me. I think the Investigating Judge was impressed by your clarity and consistency."

"There's no reason why I wouldn't be clear or consistent, it's the truth after all."

Christos smiled and nodded, "I know, but even so I thought it went very well."

Hunter sat down while Christos paced. "Don't worry, the DNA analysis will be done soon and we'll get you released. They can't proceed just on the circumstantial evidence or on statements of two known criminals. It's a shame you took Johnson's gun though. Do you know if it was that gun that was used to kill Marcos?"

"I haven't got a clue. I wasn't in the room."

"The ballistic evidence will answer that, let's hope that it show's that that gun wasn't used to kill Marcos. You said that you fired it."

"Yes when I went into Marcos place."

Christos thought, "Well we'll deal with that when we get to it. Still your story is consistent, Kate's story backs you up, and the DNA will back you up. It should be enough."

"How long will that take?"

"I'm afraid it will take a while but because of the seriousness of the case it will be hurried through."

"So what are we looking at, days, weeks?"

"It could be weeks but I hope days."

"I hope so as well, anyway what's happened to Kate?"

"She is in the same situation as you at the moment. She gave her statement yesterday, but is being detained pending further investigations, but I am not representing her and obviously I am not allowed to discuss the case with her lawyer. When I can let you know anything I will. Oh by the way they did though recover Maria's body and are going to carry out a post mortem."

"What about the others? When will they have all the evidence from them."

"That's a little odd, they are not passing on any information about that. I don't know why, I have asked, I'm sure that they'll tell us soon enough."

For a while they faced each other in silence, Christos wanted to go but could sense that Hunter didn't want to be left.

"I'm afraid I need to go, unless there's anything else you want to know."

"No, I'm sure you'll let me know when there is anything."

"I'll see you tomorrow then, in the meantime is there anything you need?"

"Just something to read, something long, I think I've got enough time on my hands to tackle something challenging." Hunter said with a smile.

Christos smiled back, "I'll see what I can get you." He went to the door and knocked, when the guard opened it Christos started to leave but paused at the door, "By the way the story is all over the press, not just here but back in the States, at this moment you and Miss Adams are a celebrity couple."

"Great." Hunter said with a tone of heavy irony.

Christos gave Hunter a reassuring smile then he was gone. Hunter got up to follow him and was accompanied by the guard back to his cell. The guard opened the cell door and Hunter went in grimacing as the heavy cell door was closed and locked. He lay down on the bed and stared at the ceiling.

Later that afternoon, the guard brought in a book with a note from Christos which said, "I bet you ten Euro that you'll be out before you've finished it." The book was War and Peace.

"I'd better be" Hunter thought, then made himself comfortable and started to read.

Hunter had plenty of time to read over the next few days. His meals were brought to him regularly and each day he met with Christos for an update on the progress of the investigation, of which there was none, but one ray of light in the gloom of his predicament was an e-mail from his employers to the effect that they would do whatever they could to support him and that he shouldn't worry about work. That at least was some reassurance and evidence to Hunter that people who were important to him believed in his innocence. The following day Christos delivered an even better piece of news. Kate had been released pending further investigations, which as Christos told him was a formality but which really meant that she had been exonerated. This was a real fillip for Hunter as it meant not only was Kate free but he hoped it might not be much longer before he himself was released.

On the fourth day Hunter was taken from the cell to the interview room. Christos was there sitting across from the detective and the Investigating Judge who gestured for Hunter to sit down which he did.

"We have the results of the DNA testing and from the ballistics. I am sure you would like to know what they say?" The question was rhetorical but still the Investigating Judge paused for dramatic effect and looked Hunter straight in the eye. "The DNA testing on the blood at the Villa Delphi, show that there was blood from three different people. Two of these samples match those taken from the bodies that were found in the premises, the third is unidentified. None of these samples match your DNA."

Hunter looked excitedly at Christos but before he could speak the Investigating Judge continued.

"The results of the ballistics examination show that both of the people whose bodies were found at the scene were shot by the guns that were found on or near their bodies. None of the injuries were caused by shoots fired from either of the guns that were found in your possession. The ballistics also confirmed that the bullet found embedded in the floor of Marcos's house was fired from the gun that was in your possession. Furthermore we found a number of passports at the villa with a number of different names but your photograph, or at least a photograph that looked like you. We checked the visa stamps against those on your passport which showed that you were in Germany at the same time that the holder of the other passports was in

Hong Kong. Your employer has confirmed that you were in Germany at that time." She paused to let the importance of what she had just said sink in. "The photograph on the other passports though is uncannily similar to yours. Considering this evidence, your story and its consistency with that of Miss Adams, allied to the detailed records of your movements over the last year given to us by your employer we have to conclude that you have been telling the truth and that you do indeed have a doppelganger. Someone who is unknown to us and unknown to the FBI. Someone who we would dearly like to find."

As the Investigating Judge paused, Christos spoke, "So this means you will be releasing my client?"

"Yes, we will overlook the other minor charges," then to Hunter "we're going to let you go now but we would like you to make yourself available to answer any further questions."

"Thanks but what does that mean, am I free to return to the states?"

"Yes, but should we find this other man, Johnson, you may be required to return to give evidence in a trial, we are also looking for the third man, Johnson's other accomplice, and will be prosecuting the two who worked for Marcos. We are also conducting an investigation into the local Police department as we suspect that there may have been some collusion. So as you can see we have a long way to go in this case."

Then the detective smiled stood up and held out his hand. Hunter stood up and shook the detective's hand.

"We owe you our thanks." The detective continued, "The head

you recovered was of great value it would have been a tragedy if it had been taken from Greece and gone into some private collection, thank you for recovering it."

Hunter was taken aback.

"You're free to go." The detective added.

"Come on," said Christos, "we've got some paperwork to do, then we can go."

After the paperwork had been completed, Hunter was given back his own clothes which had been washed and pressed, then accompanied by his copy of War and Peace he was ready to leave. Christos was waiting for him.

"You owe me ten euro." He said and they laughed.

"I'm afraid you'll have to wait," Hunter said, "until I can get to a bank."

"Don't worry, I'm just glad that it was concluded so quickly. Now before we leave, you need to be prepared to answer some more questions."

"I thought they had everything they needed?"

"No not the police or the investigating judge, the press."

"I hadn't thought of that."

"Yes there's a bit of a mob. Just keep the answers short and to the point, but I'll be with you to field anything difficult."

"Ok let's do it."

With that they walked out through the police station doors to be greeted by a mass of journalists, photographers and television news cameras. They were held back by an outnumbered group of uniformed police but surged forward as soon as they saw Hunter.

He was bombarded with questions, all of which he answered directly and concisely, occasionally interrupted by Christos who added further detail, or who batted the question away on legal grounds. The impromptu press conference lasted fifteen minutes at which point the assembled mass seemed to be satisfied and Christos was able to lead Hunter unhindered to a waiting car.

"There's someone waiting to see you." Christos said.

"Kate?" Hunter asked.

Christos nodded in affirmation.

They drove a short distance to a quiet green square in which there was an outdoor cafe. Hunter gave Christos, who insisted he needed to get on, his thanks and got out of the car. He stood for a moment, eyes closed, looking upwards feeling the warmth of the sun on his face. It felt good, for a while he had feared that he might not know this sensation for a long time, but now he was away from the police station and the journalists Hunter felt a huge weight had been lifted from his shoulders, he felt free. His stay had been a short one and had served to reinforce his opinion that he never wanted to end up in jail. Now he wanted a good breakfast, orange juice, coffee, fresh bread, eggs, a simple pleasure just like the feeling of the sun, and to see Kate.

He looked around and saw the cafe, then he saw Kate sitting there looking at him. She smiled and waved. Hunter felt a wave of pure joy at seeing her. He crossed the street and by the time he reached her she was standing waiting for him. They threw themselves into each other's arms and held each other tightly for a long time. When they broke off, Kate looked up into his eyes then kissed him.

"I'm pleased to see you." She said.

"Are you ok?" He asked in reply.

Kate nodded. "Yes I'm fine, come on let's sit down and get some coffee."

They sat down and Hunter ordered his breakfast, which was quickly delivered, he sipped the coffee and looked at Kate, who seemed to him even more beautiful than before, all felt right with the world.

They sat there for some time, each relating to the other what had happened to them at the police station. Although Kate had been released she wasn't completely free, there would be an official inquest and it was still possible that she may face a charge of manslaughter but the police had accepted that Maria's death had been a result of her own actions and that Kate had been acting in self defence, they wouldn't be pressing any charges but it was down to the investigating magistrate.

"Are you worried?" Hunter asked

"I suppose I should be, but somehow I think after what has happened I should be thankful that I survived. I've just got to take it a day at a time, get back to my work and deal with the consequences when I have to."

"If it comes to it I'll make sure you get the best representation."

"Thanks." Then she flashed a smile at Hunter that said the subject was closed and it was time to move on. "Have you finished." She asked.

Hunter nodded. "Yes that was great."

"No cigarette?"

"You know I'd almost forgotten about smoking, I think I've just been cold turkey, no I'm back on the no smoking wagon again."

"Good, now I'm going to take you to meet someone."

"That sounds mysterious."

"It's not meant to be, but I'll keep it as a surprise."

They paid the bill and walked off through the streets and into the old town to the archaeological museum.

"It wasn't really my plan to spend the day inside looking at old relics." Hunter said.

"We won't be long come on." Kate said smiling.

She took Hunter's hand and led him through the museum to

Stafis's office. She knocked on the door and went in. There on the desk was the head with Stafis and another man, Professor Gounaris from Athens huddled around it, Stafis brush in hand cleaning away dirt that had accumulated over many years. Kate coughed and the two men looked up.

"Kate, you're here, good," Stafis said, "and is this the man we have to thank for recovering this outstanding object."

"It is." Kate replied.

Stafis approached Hunter, took his hand and shook it vigorously. "Thank you, thank you very much." He said.

Hunter grinned broadly, taken aback by the old man's enthusiasm. "You're welcome." He said, "although I didn't do it for altruistic reasons, just to save my own skin, and Kate's."

"Whatever your motivation, the result is that you have saved a historically significant and beautiful object for Greece."

Hunter extracted himself from Stafis's grip and all four of them gathered around the head examining it from all angles. "Even I must admit, it's not bad." Hunter said.

"Not bad?" Kate exclaimed, "It's the single most important artefact to be found in oh, I don't know how many years, professor?"

"We've a lot of work to do yet but I can confidently say that nothing like this has come to light in oh..." He looked at professor Gounaris "what would you say fifty years?" Professor Gounaris shrugged and nodded in reply. "Yes fifty years," Stafis continued, "a lot of work to do" he said absentmindedly going back to cleaning. "A lot of work."

This was their cue to leave. Hunter stopped at the door and looked back. "Professor." He said. Both Stafis and Professor Gounaris looked up. "Take care of it, it's caused a lot of trouble to a lot of people, and if you don't mind me saying, it is beautiful and I understand it is significant, but I hope I never see it again."

Kate pulled Hunter out of the room shutting the door quietly behind her. "What do you want to do now." Kate asked.

"Have the holiday I came here for."

CHAPTER 8

After they'd left the museum they returned to Hunter's hotel where they picked up the rest of his stuff and he was able finally to check out officially and pay the bill. After his arrest Christos had cancelled Hunter's room and his belongings had been held in storage. Then they returned to Kate's house where they could relax and Hunter could unwind after his ordeal.

It was a perfect day and Hunter was happy to lie out in the sun intermittently dozing, reading, swimming and eating an assortment of snacks that Kate kept him supplied with. It was the sort of thing Hunter had planned when he had decided to take his vacation on Rhodes but the experience was enhanced by Kate's presence. He felt so lucky to have met her and could not imagine how he would repay her for everything she had done for him or the ordeal she had suffered and for which he felt responsible. There was something else nagging at him. They had become very close over the last week but were yet to make love. Hunter wanted to very much not just out of lust and the satisfaction of that most basic bodily function but also out of love. His feelings for Kate were so strong that he wanted to show them physically and utterly but those feelings also made him cautious about suggesting anything or making a move. With Kate he wouldn't want to act inappropriately and he didn't want to do anything that may jeopardise their relationship. But every time she came into his sight his hormones started to get the better of him and he had to dive for the pool.

As the day slipped into evening and Hunter slipped into a large gin and tonic he felt contented and relaxed. Kate sat adjacent to him with her own drink and they talked about anything other than what had happened to them since they first met. It was comfortable, un-strained and easy. They talked about whether to eat out or stay there and cook, both content with either solution but as they neared the bottom of their glasses the decision was made to eat at a small village restaurant that was close by.

The restaurant was really a taverna frequented mainly by locals but supplemented by the odd tourist who was exploratory enough to head off the beaten track and find somewhere different. The meal was simple but excellent dolmos, kalamari, olives, and salad, all washed down with the local retzina.

Once they were back at Kate's the air was starting to cool so they went inside and before anything could be said they were in each other's arms and shortly afterwards in Kate's bed.

The next morning Hunter woke to the sight of Kate's sun-tanned shoulder poking out from the sheet and her blonde hair cascading over the pillow and he felt himself to be a very lucky man indeed. He slipped out of bed as quietly as possible and pulled on his shorts before going to the kitchenette and making coffee.

Returning to the bedroom he placed the mugs of coffee on the floor and slipped back into the bed but although he tried not to disturb her Kate rolled over and looked up at him. He smiled "I've got you some coffee." He said but before the words were out of his mouth Kate had pulled him down to her and they were making love again.

When they had finished, the coffee was cold and Hunter felt

less inclined to get up and make some more. He lay on his back with Kate lying close to him, her head nestled on his shoulder, his arm around her. She looked up at him. "What are we going to do?" She asked.

Hunter smiled, "in life or just today?"

"I was thinking of somewhere in between!"

Hunter didn't understand. "What do you mean?"

"There are so many loose ends. I know the Police are trying to sort it out, but isn't there anything we could do?"

"I think it is probably best to leave it alone. We're dealing with dangerous and ruthless people, I would suggest that we satisfy ourselves with the fact that we are still alive and were not badly hurt, and that we recovered the head."

Kate rested her head back on Hunter's shoulder but he could sense that she hadn't given up on the subject. After a pause she lifted Hunter's arm off her and sat up, then got out of bed. "Come on lazy, I'll make the coffee then we can put our heads together."

Hunter watched her go then dropped his head back on the pillow. "What's going to be next?" He thought.

After he had showered and dressed he walked out into the garden, where Kate was waiting with the coffee and a tray of breakfast.

Hunter sat down took a cup and sipped it slowly, waiting for

Kate, who looked like she was bursting to say something. She couldn't hold back for long before the words burst out. "I think we have to find Johnson."

Hunter looked at her and shook his head, "but why? What can we possibly gain by finding Johnson?"

Kate looked serious and was forthright, "we can prove once and for all that he is not you, and we can find out where the head came from."

"The police know he is not me and to be quite frank I don't need to know where the head came from, I've had quite enough of the whole thing, I just want to stay for a few days, to relax, then get on a plane back to the states and get on with my life!"

Kate's face flushed, she was angry, "Oh thanks, so this means nothing to you?"

Hunter stumbled over his words as he realised what he had said, "No, of course it means something, but, well you have your PhD to finish and I, well I can't just stay here can I? It doesn't mean..." he pulled himself together, "Look Kate, we've just been through an intense and traumatic experience, and I think the best way to get over it is to get on with our lives, so why can't we just enjoy this time together without any complications and then see what the future brings?"

Kate's expression didn't change and despite the heat the atmosphere was decidedly frosty. After an agonising pause Kate looked around at Hunter her face determined and without it's usual softness. "You're right of course, I don't know what I was thinking. I've got work to do, so if you don't mind after I've got ready I'll drop you off in town and you can find yourself a hotel and get on with your life."

Hunter's protests fell on closed ears as Kate got up and went into the house. He didn't follow her, he thought it best not to but instead sat there looking at the ripples on the surface of the swimming pool water and cursed himself, this was not what he wanted, not what he wanted at all.

Understanding women was probably not one of Hunter's strong points. He had been brought up to treat women as equals and although his experiences had not changed this opinion it had taught him that women were different.

He wasn't shy of women, he enjoyed their company and had through his life drifted in and out of relationships some more serious than others but none that lasted. His focus had been on his career, he had never been interested in marriage or children, he didn't want to close himself off from opportunities and his whole self image was of a single man, independent, self contained, happy in his own skin without the need of a permanent partner to boost his self esteem. At the same time he had a romantic side and in his dreams would find that perfect person with whom there was an unspoken but very true connection.

As he sat looking at the ripples he pondered his attitudes and questioned whether it was time for him to change. He was making a huge assumption but maybe Kate was the one. With all that had happened since they met he hadn't taken time to consider her seriously as a partner. Their relationship had been born from a turbulent and dramatic situation it had been a whirlwind affair and had he even considered it, he would have concluded that that was all it was. Kate would be a wonderful memory to accompany what would probably be the most dramatic time of his life. He would return to normality and Kate would be a romantic figure in the past. Something though was nagging at him, it was a sensation he wasn't used to and didn't want to admit to, inside himself he knew that he didn't want this to be the end of their affair. He got up and went into the house where Kate was dressed and packing some things into her bag. Hunter approached her and she stopped what she was doing and looked straight at him but didn't smile. Hunter held her by the shoulders pulled her toward him and kissed her. Kate didn't resist but he could feel the tension in her body and she didn't kiss him back.

"I'm sorry" he said, "this does mean something to me, you mean a lot to me, sometimes I talk without thinking, please don't be angry with me."

Hunter felt Kate's shoulders relax and she managed a little smile.

"You were right, we've both been under a huge strain, stay here, have your holiday and let's see what happens."

Hunter was relieved, "can you spare some time to spend it with me?"

"I've got work to do, you know and because of you I'm behind, so I'm going to work but we can have the evening together."

"Yes, I don't want to interfere with your work, are you going to do it here?"

"No, I'm going to the museum," then with a cheeky look "There'll be fewer distractions." With that she pulled him toward her and kissed him with passion.

"Do you want to go somewhere? I can drop you off."

"No I'll hang out here and see you when you get back, but don't be too late, I want to take you out to the best restaurant you know."

"OK it's a date." Kate picked up her bag and went to leave, she paused in the door "oh and don't talk to any strange men!" and with that she was gone.

Almost immediately Hunter missed her presence, and the nagging feeling returned. He went back out to the pool, stripped off and jumped in. His feet touched the bottom, he held himself there and looked up at the sunlight reflecting on the disturbed surface of the water. He let himself float up to the surface and took a deep breath before swimming to the other end. He swam back and forth for some time, it felt good to him to use his body, to exercise. Eventually he tired and rested on the edge of the pool his chin resting on his folded arms. He closed his eyes and felt the warmth of the sun on his shoulders while he thought happy thoughts, mainly about Kate. He ducked down again into the water and swam a few more lengths before pulling himself out of the water and lying by the pool letting the sun dry him. The heat was building and as it became more soporific Hunter gradually fell into a light doze. A sudden gust of wind disturbed him and he came around momentarily unsure of his surroundings. He sat up and took in the scene then realising that the sun had become more intense went into the house to find some sun cream. He got himself a cold beer from the fridge, after all he was on holiday, then checked the bathroom for some sun-cream. Once he was suitably protected he went back outside and sat down again by the pool, but he couldn't settle. There were too many questions that needed answering, predominantly, where was Johnson and, he decided more importantly, what would happen with his relationship with Kate?

It was the second of these questions that bothered him most. He hadn't experienced the nagging feeling in his guts that he had first felt that morning when he had thought that he had blown it with her. He didn't like it and didn't want to give it its name, love. He'd always managed to control these feelings in the past preserving his independence, but now although he was loath to admit it, Kate had got to him, he wanted to be in her company, no, needed to be with her and above all he wanted to look after her, protect her, and make her happy. He snapped himself out of this line of thinking and sucked down his beer while he got up and paced up and down by the pool.

He needed to get out, he should have probably taken Kate up on her offer to drop him somewhere where he would be distracted from his thoughts, instead he was stuck so he determined to go for a walk. He went back into the house and searched around for a map, but all he could find was a road map which wouldn't be much help if he was walking except that Kate had conveniently marked the location of the house so at least he knew where he was. He wrote a quick note for Kate that he left on the kitchen counter then dressed and taking the map, some money and a bottle of water with him, locked up the house and set off.

He started by looking around the perimeter of the garden looking for a path but finding none walked down to the road. He set off east so that the sun wouldn't be in his face then changed his mind and headed west, so that when he was returning he'd have the sun behind him. The road stretched out into the distance, a heat haze rising from the traffic-less black surface and Hunter hoped that there would be a path somewhere soon.

It wasn't long before he found a track leading south off the road. The ground rose ahead of him and he could see that the track wound uphill through clumps of trees over what appeared to be uncultivated land. It was just what he needed as he hoped that from the high ground he may be able to plot some circular walk. The path followed a not too steep gradient as it wandered up the hillside, it was hot but a stiffening breeze kept Hunter tolerably cool. He walked at a gentle pace and took the opportunity of shade from the randomly dispersed trees to stop for a moment and take in the expanding view. Rounding an outcrop of limestone Hunter reached what he had imagined would be the top of the hill only to find out that it was a false summit behind which was an olive grove beyond which the hillside continued to rise. He looked up at the barren sun-parched hillside and questioned whether he really wanted to continue. He could not make out any discernible path and was becoming thirsty, but now he felt determined to reach the summit of the hill even though this had not been his original intention.

He entered the olive grove and while he could, enjoyed the cool of the shade before emerging into the sunlight, the heat of which was magnified by its reflection from the numerous boulders that scattered across the slope of the hill. There was no path so he headed directly upwards, over the smaller rocks, weaving between the bigger outcrops. He was soon sweating profusely and wishing he had brought some water with him but at the same time he was enjoying the effort and in a perverse way enjoying the hardship.

The summit came almost unexpectedly, it wasn't a peak, but a rounded hilltop from where he could see both the east and west coasts of the island and could look north over the plain to Rhodes town and beyond to the coast of Turkey. He sat down and his shirt stuck to him, the breeze quickly cooling him down, so he took his shirt off and laid it on a rock to dry while he went a little way down the lee side of the hill where the breeze was not so strong and let the warmth of the sun dry him while he sat and looked down toward Rhodes town. His thoughts wandered to Kate, who was somewhere down there, and what would happen when, in a few days he returned to the States. Would the relationship last? Did he want it to last? He tried to visualise them together back home, imagining what their domestic life would be like together and how things would be when they were old. The images he created in his mind were good, he could see them being together and it dawned on him that this was a happier vision of his future than that he had always imagined of a single old man going about his business.

He felt content, he could see the future and it looked good. He gazed out at the landscape not really taking in what he was seeing, basking in the pleasant pictures he had created in his mind. Eventually he became fidgety, he really did need something to drink, so he recovered his now dry shirt and took a closer look at the near landscape. He couldn't see the road directly below him due to the topography of the hill side but not far to the east he could see a small village which must have been on the same road and he decide that rather than just retrace his steps he would head to the village in the hope that there would be a bar or cafe where he could get something to drink and wile away what remained of the afternoon before walking or hopefully hitching a lift back down the road to Kate's house. He scanned the slope that lead down to the village and plotted a route around what looked like it could be a small cliff and between the inevitable olive groves. The terrain was rough under foot and as he proceeded carefully down the slope, it occurred to him that, especially as no one knew where he was, it would not be a good place to twist an ankle or have an accident.

He skirted around what turned out to be more than a small cliff and was soon working his way around the first of the olive groves. Now he was off the hill and in the trees on the flat navigation was harder and he had to retrace his steeps a few times to avoid climbing over the higher of the dry-stone walls. Eventually he came out of the trees onto the road a few hundred yards away from the start of the village. He walked briskly to the centre where there was a small open area and exactly what he was looking for, a cafe with a few tables and chairs outside in the shade of an awning. He went straight in and found himself the only customer, the owner sitting behind the bar listening to the radio. He managed to order both water and a beer and having gulped the water down immediately took the beer outside and positioned himself in the shade with a view of the road and the deserted village. A few cars passed in platoons of two or three and the major excitement was provided by the appearance of a tractor towing a trailer piled high with loose straw, the driver, his hat so closely attached to his head it appeared to be part of his body, a cigarette clamped in his mouth, his face and forearms dark tanned from a lifetime of exposure to the Aegean sun.

Hunter finished his beer and for once in his life didn't know what to do with himself. Usually even on vacation he had a schedule in his mind but on this day there was nothing he had to do so he headed back up the road toward Kate's house. Due to the heat the walk felt longer than it really was and he was pleased to arrive back. He drank a couple of glasses of water and went straight to the pool diving in and feeling immediately revived by the cool of the water. He spent the rest of the afternoon swimming, sunbathing and reading, having a holiday. So absorbed was he in the job of relaxation he didn't realise how much time had passed until he noticed that the shadows had lengthened and the light had changed. It was rapidly heading toward sunset and Hunter wondered how long it would be until Kate returned. He was looking forward to seeing her and having dinner together, he was anticipating good food, good wine and a romantic evening. He showered, and changed, then mixed himself a gin and tonic before sitting down by the pool with his book to await Kate's return. It was gone seven and he assumed that she would not be long. When she still wasn't back by eight he was not just disappointed but starting to get angry, not to say hungry. After that the time dragged and he abandoned all prospect of the evening he had imagined. Then he started to worry. He had tried her mobile phone several times but it went straight to answer phone. At first he had left a gently enquiring message as to when she expected to return. Then he had left a more urgent message, his concern evident in the tone of his voice. Nine came and went and it was closer to ten when his mobile rang.

CHAPTER 9

Hunter held back from answering with "and where the hell are you?" and was glad that he did because it wasn't Kate on the other end of the line. Instead it was a man's voice that he heard, a voice he had heard before and believed he would never hear again. It was Johnson.

"You don't have to say anything," Johnson started, "in fact it will be better if you say nothing."

Hunter listened.

"I expect that you have guessed by now but your girlfriend is here, with me." He paused for effect, "now I need your passport so I suggest you bring it to me."

Hunter knew that Johnson was telling the truth, after all Kate hadn't come back and Johnson was talking on her phone but he felt he had to make a token protest. "How do I know you're telling the truth, let me speak to her!"

Johnson laughed, "Come on do we really have to go through all that?"

Hunter didn't reply and through the phone he heard some shuffling and then in the background he heard Kate's voice, "John! John!" followed by noises that suggested she had been restrained from saying any more.

"You'd better not hurt her." Hunter said surprising himself

with the determination in his voice. "What do you want me to do?"

"Stay where you are and don't contact anyone. We'll let you know where and when." Then the phone went dead.

Hunter looked at the phone for a few moments then screamed and shouted out a string of expletives. Then having got the tension out started planning for what was to come. He had to save Kate but he was damned if he was going to help Johnson escape. He had been sure that he had seen the last of Johnson now he was back to haunt him. He had to prepare. But how?

First he got his passport and placed it on the breakfast bar then searched around the kitchen for some sort of weapon that he could conceal. The larger knives were out of the question, he needed something smaller. Eventually he found a small sharp knife which he placed on the side with the intention of carrying it hidden in his sock. He then had something to eat, he didn't know what would happen or when he would eat again so he needed to stock up. He made a meal of cheese, cold meat and bread and against his inclination left the beer in the fridge and instead drank several glasses of water. He also placed a full bottle next to the knife. He then brewed up a pot of strong coffee on the assumption that he would get the call soon.

He put on his Harrington jacket put his passport in the inside pocket and put the water and a jumper in a plastic bag. Then he had an idea and searched the house for a torch which he found in the obvious place near the front door. He put the torch in the bag along with a map of the island. There was little else he could think of to do so he wrapped the blade of the knife loosely in some toilet paper and experimented with positioning in his sock finding that the best position was at the back of his right foot down along the outside of his Achilles. Now prepared he sat down and sipped at the coffee as ready as he could be for what was to come.

Hunter was lost in thought when he heard the car, and was immediately wide awake his senses alert, as ready as he could be for what was about to come. He stood up and grabbed his bag then stood by the door feeling the knife in his sock uncomfortably rubbing against his leg. He heard the car make a three point turn so that it would be pointing down the driveway toward the road. He then heard the door open and unexpectedly light footsteps approaching the house. Hunter tensed and was surprised to hear a quiet voice outside the door.

"Mr Hunter could you come outside please?"

Hunter cautiously opened the door and was confronted by the old man he had met at Lindos. He was so taken aback he neither moved or said anything.

"Please can you come with me?" The old man politely asked.

Hunter stepped forward but before he had closed the door the old man coughed lightly to attract his attention. "I'm afraid you can't bring that bag." He said.

Hunter had recovered from his surprise, "I've only got some water and a jumper" He said.

The old man shook his head apologetically and Hunter hoping that by leaving the bag he would avoid being searched chucked the bag back into the house and closed the door.

"Now raise your arms above your head."

Hunter complied and the old man patted him down but crucially it was a cursory search and Hunter's concealed knife went unfound. He breathed a silent thank you and followed the old man to the car, surprised that he had come by himself. As if reading Hunter's mind the old man answered the unspoken question with an implied threat. "You won't try anything, don't forget the girl." Hunter nodded and got into the passenger seat of the car.

For a small island like Rhodes the journey was a long one, they drove out to the West Coast and then headed south before turning into the hills on a small twisting road. Hunter had the distinct impression that the old man was not taking the direct route and despite his attempts to follow the route, in the dark and with his lack of knowledge of the island Hunter soon became disoriented.

They came down from the hills and headed south along the East Coast. The road was deserted, as was the surrounding countryside, which was flat farmland, the moon light reflected from the sea to their left and Hunter felt they were a long way from civilisation. They passed the odd building and through one small village before winding up into a further set of hills. Cresting the hills Hunter could see the sea below, the road heading down to an isthmus which formed the southern tip of the island. Hunter knew they were approaching journey's end and tried to mentally prepare himself for the moment of truth that he knew was about to come. But how could he prepare? He had to deal with the situation as it unfolded, there could be no premeditated plan.

They were soon down at sea level again and rather than driving onto the isthmus the old man turned off onto a rocky track. They made slow progress bumping up and down, the car's suspension only partly absorbing the impact of the ruts and loose stones, greater impacts sending both the old man and Hunter bouncing off their seats. The old man looked at Hunter with a half apologetic half-mischievous smile which caused Hunter to wonder why someone who appeared to be so polite and civilised would be mixed up with someone as ruthless as Johnson.

The track came to an end at a small cove where a couple of fishing boats were pulled up away from the water's edge on the shingle beach. Ahead of them was a rocky promontory and above an escarpment of earth and loose stones. Hunter got out of the car and the old man did likewise then pointed toward the promontory. "That way." He said. Hunter walked across the beach past the boats and up on to the rocks of the promontory pausing to look back and see if the old man was following. He was right behind and indicated with a wave for Hunter to continue around. It turned out that there was a wave cut platform and it was easy to walk around, the sea lapping mere feet below, the promontory forming a barrier above. It took just a few minutes to 'round the promontory before the old man put his hand on Hunter's shoulder to stop him.

"It's me! We're here!" The old man shouted.

"Come on in!" Came the reply which Hunter recognised as coming from Johnson.

On hearing the voice Hunter saw a cave with a low light faintly emanating from its entrance.

"Go on." The old man said gesticulating toward the cave mouth. Hunter approached it gingerly, unsure what scene would greet him when he entered. He rounded the edge of the cave and went in. The cave bent round to the right and it was from beyond this bend that the source of the light and, Hunter expected, Johnson were to be found. Even though his focus was on what was to come he had to admit that it was a great hiding place, so remote and so well hidden that it could only be found by those who knew of it's existence. The old man followed close behind as Hunter made his way cautiously around the bend in the cave and into the light.

There he saw Kate, gagged and tied to a chair. As soon as she saw Hunter she writhed in a symbolic show of defiance intended for Hunter, her eyes sparkled with energy and Hunter knew she was ok. Next to her was Johnson, who sat on a box, gun in hand, and grinned at Hunter when he appeared and laughed at Kate's struggle. The cave at this point was shallow, and the only other objects in it were a gas lamp, a gas stove with a saucepan, a half-full bin bag and a black rucksack. Johnson was ready to go and didn't intend to leave any sign of his presence.

"I thought you were dead." Hunter said.

"At one point so did I, but luckily, for me if not for you, nothing important was damaged, but I'll wear the scars all my life. Anyway I haven't brought you here for a friendly chat. Throw your passport over to me!"

Hunter was hesitant, his passport was his only bargaining chip but he couldn't see any choice, so he took it from his pocket and threw it onto the floor just in front of Johnson causing him to have to stand and bend over to pick it up. When he did so, Hunter could see that it caused Johnson some pain, his wounds must not have been completely healed. Hunter wanted to point this out, make some remark, but now was not the time for provocation.

Johnson sat back down again and resting his gun in his lap flicked through Hunter's passport, stopping at the page with the photograph. "Excellent, no one will be able to tell the difference." He put the passport in a pocket on the top flap of the rucksack and pointing the gun at Hunter signalled for him to go over to where Kate was tied up.

Hunter followed the signal and when he was close gave Kate a big wink and a smile in an attempt to reassure her, it was then that he felt the bullet hit him followed in an infinitesimal delay by the sound of the shot magnified by the confined space echoing all around the chamber. As Hunter fell to the ground, Kate, underneath her gag screamed and tried fervently to loosen her bindings. Then the second shot rang out and Hunter felt it hit him again then as he looked up at Kate for what he thought would be the last time, he passed out.

When he came to, daylight was forcing its way into the cave. He looked at his watch, it was 10.30. He didn't move at first but took in the scene from his recumbent position. The chair was gone as was Kate. He moved a little and felt a searing pain in his midriff and another in his shoulder so he lay for a little longer summoning up the courage to bear the pain and sit up. He did so by first rolling onto his good shoulder and then doing a semi-press-up until he could roll his legs in front of him and sit gasping as he did so with the stabs of pain in his waist and shoulder. "Kate! What had happened to Kate?" His mind screamed at him and he knew that he could not sit there and feel sorry for himself. He felt his shoulder and to his surprise underneath his bloodstained shirt there was a dressing, it was the same with the wound in his waist, "So they hadn't meant to kill me. But why shoot me?"

He managed to stand up and staggered out of the cave to be dazzled by the bright sunlight. He paused a moment until his eyes had accustomed themselves to the light then cautiously made his way around the headland, pausing and leaning against the rocks every few steps to gain his breath and wait for the pain to subside before starting again and continuing until the pain again became to much. When he reached the beach it was as he had expected, deserted except for the boats that had been there the night before. He remembered how far it had been along the track from the road the night before and considered that it was too far for him to walk. Instead he sat down by the water's edge leant on a rock, looked out to the sea and waited for whom he did not know, he just hoped one of the fishermen who owned the boats would come along.

He gazed out at the horizon and thought about what had happened. Uppermost in his mind was his concern for Kate and his guilt for involving her. It was a cliché but he really thought that if something had happened to her he really would not be able to forgive himself, he just hoped that they had released her, but something in the back of his mind nagged at him, a feeling that it was just not that simple, an ominous feeling that not all was well. Where was she? What was happening to her? He tried to put himself in Johnson's mind. He wanted to get off the island, this he would do illegally, a boat over to Turkey, that part was easy, but if he wanted to travel further afield he needed a passport and Hunter's was ready made, so that way he could travel straight onward, but to where? The States was

Hunter's best guess, but how long would that take? A bus to Istanbul must take fifteen or sixteen hours so he would need twenty four hours to be sure of his escape, surely he could have just left Hunter and Kate tied up in the cave for that time, no one would have found them and then he could have let the authorities know they were there. Hunter just couldn't work out why he'd been shot in the first place and as he was shot why he had not been killed and why take Kate?

He stared out at the open sea, his mind totally absorbed in the problem. The lapping of the water and the warmth of the sun, the sheer peace of the place soothed him and as he felt himself relaxing into a semi-trance like state he realised why Johnson had shot him and at the same time his fatal flaw. He snapped himself from his relaxed state and made to stand up. The pain shot through his waist and his shoulder once again and he noticed that his shirt was now stained with blood. The dressing was not up to holding the flow back when he moved, but move he must. He was probably already too late but he had to get back, get to the police and save Kate. He steeled himself and started up the track.

His progress was slow and he stopped at every opportunity to rest in what little shade he could find, his mouth was parched and now the bloodstain was growing. He forced himself on until he was on the point of collapse then sat in the shade of a boulder and tried to recover his strength.

He didn't realise that he had passed out until he woke up. Two policemen were crouching next to him and seeing Hunter's eyes open, one of them offered him a bottle of water. Hunter drank it down and in his desperation spilt some down himself. He followed the line of the water down to his waist and saw that his shirt was now mainly red the dried blood forming an amorphous stain that spread from just below his chest to his trousers the waist band of which was also red. The policemen helped him up and into their car and after making a radio call drove him slowly back up the track.

"Kate, you've got to find Kate!" Hunter insisted desperation in his voice. The policemen looked at each other and their exchange of expression told Hunter all he needed to know.

An ambulance was waiting at the main road and Hunter was transferred into it. They set off immediately and while a paramedic cut off Hunter's shirt and started to clean him up, a policeman sat implacably watching. The man seemed oblivious to what was really going on and his expression of dumb insolence riled Hunter. He wanted to swear at him to shout, to make him realise the anguish and pain that he was feeling, make him realise how pathetic his world was how there was a greater world out there which at that moment Hunter felt had been destroyed. He had truly lost his innocence, an innocence that he had not previously realised he possessed but which he wished he could regain. For him there would be no happy ending, he would live his life in guilt and a state of emptiness that comes when you lose the person you love, you admire, who doesn't deserve to die and you believe that you were the cause, for Hunter knew that Kate was dead.

When they arrived at the hospital Hunter was x-rayed then left waiting while the doctors decided on his treatment. All the time the policeman kept his silent watch but now Hunter's anger had evaporated and been replaced by a deep melancholy, the fight had gone and he didn't care what happened any more.

It turned out that one bullet had passed clean through his oblique just above his pelvis and had missed any vital organs, the other was lodged in his shoulder it had gone in through the top of his chest scraping his collarbone and lodging against his shoulder blade. The damage was not serious but they operated immediately removing the bullet and stitching him up in both places. They had given him a general anaesthetic and while Hunter lay unconscious in his hospital bed he had the most vivid dreams. At first he dreamt of Kate by the pool in the sun, they were happy, he felt in love, he held her in his arms and it felt even better than the reality. Then the dream changed, a huge wave swept over them and all of a sudden they were out in a storm tossed sea being thrown around in the waves, Hunter desperately trying to reach Kate, he went under, then when he surfaced she was gone. He screamed and screamed then woke up in the hospital, damp with perspiration, his shoulder bandaged and a new policeman sitting watching.

It was the next day that the police inspector came to see him, he was accompanied by Christos the lawyer. They sat by Hunter's bed and Christos tried to force a reassuring smile but was prevented by his own discomfort at the knowledge that he had and Hunter was about to learn.

The inspector was more matter of fact, but started with some niceties. "How are you feeling today?"

Hunter gave the required answer, "not too bad thank you."

Then the inspector started for real. "First I need to tell you that we do know that you are Hunter and not Johnson. We obviously had the previous DNA samples and as a matter of urgency we have had yours matched against them. This is something the criminal Johnson overlooked. How he could have made that mistake we do not know, we can only conclude that he imagined that we couldn't get a DNA sample from the house where he was shot and didn't know that we had managed to. It's a mistake that both caused you your injuries and quite possibly saved your life. You see his intention was for us to believe that you were Johnson and had been hiding in that cave since the first incident, that's why he shot you but didn't kill you, it was stupid really, your wounds were fresh and his would have been partially healed but I suppose he thought that you would die there before we found you, and you may well have done if we hadn't received the phone call."

Hunter interrupted. "What phone call?"

"It was anonymous of course but told us that Johnson was hiding in a cave on the south coast. We didn't know where this cave was but we sent men down all the roads along the south and as luck had it we found you. We would not have found the cave so quickly if you had still been there, you did the right thing to get out." The inspector paused, all three of them knew what was coming next but it still had to be said, "Your friend Miss Adams was not quite so lucky." The use of the adverb quite, annoyed Hunter, she was the opposite of luckily, fully, moderately, quite. "I'm sorry to inform you that her body was found on a beach not far from where we found you, we will carry out a post mortem but it appears that she drowned." Hunter's face tightened, it was the news he had expected but nonetheless it was still painful to hear it.

He tried to hold his emotions in check but his voice broke as he asked, "Why? Why did he kill Kate?"

"Only Johnson knows for sure, this is all speculation, but we think because if his plan was to work he couldn't leave any loose ends, and Kate had seen you both together, it seems absurd, but I'm afraid that is all I can tell you at the moment."

"What about Johnson?" Hunter asked.

The detective shrugged, "We assume he is in Turkey, we have informed Interpol and the airports have his description and the fact that he is travelling on your passport, until he makes a move there is little anyone can do, but he made a huge mistake with you and Miss Adams, he'll make a mistake again and then he'll pay for his crimes."

The detective got up to leave then stopped, "I hope you make a good recovery." With which he left.

Christos had remained silent while the detective was talking, now he spoke. "I'm very sorry about Miss Adams. Were you very close?"

Images of Kate flashed through Hunter's mind and he started to sob, quietly at first, then as the emotion rose from deep inside uncontrollably. Christos put a reassuring hand on Hunter's shoulder and let him cry. When the sobs subsided and Hunter had wiped the tears from his face, he forced a smile at Christos, "I didn't know it until now, but I've never been as close to anyone in my life, and I never will be."